The Memoir of Jake Weedsong

A Novel

THE MEMOIR OF JAKE WEEDSONG

A NOVEL

Timothy Schell

Pax

SERVING HOUSE BOOKS

The Memoir of Jake Weedsong

ISBN: 978-0-9826921-7-2

Cover photo © Wtolenaars | Dreamstime.com

Author photo by Maya Schell

Serving House Books logo by Barry Lereng Wilmont

Published by Serving House Books
Copenhagen and Florham Park, NJ

www.servinghousebooks.com

First Serving House Books Edition 2011

For Sachiko and Maya

As I sit here and type in my office in my home in Banks, Oregon, I hear my wife Etsuko vacuuming the living room. We had a rather late dinner party last night at which two of us, my good friend and colleague Gunnar Hoagart and I, finished off the dinner with a bottle of Calvados, a bold if not rare effort on our part. I should, I suppose, mention the menu: a salad with thin strips of smoked goose with a light raspberry vinaigrette, braised lamb shanks and country potatoes, and several bottles of our own Pinot gris, both fruity and pebbly and so aromatic as to call in the doves. Now, on the goose, this: Gunnar and I had been out hunting the day before and each of us shot an eight or nine pound cackler. After quartering mine, I soaked the pieces in a rum-based brine for twelve hours and then smoked it for twelve more with a fine cherry and alder mix. The finished product was nothing less than sublime. Still, though, there is the sentimental side of me which cries at the image of that arm of geese flying back over us looking for their fallen mate, and I wonder why it is that I have such an atavistic need to kill birds, fish and mammals for it is not because I need to do so to survive. Yet in landing a twelve pound steelhead on the banks of the Wilson River, I strut and girdle up my loins in an imbecilic fashion reserved for slightly less than fifty percent of the world's population.

I stray from the task at hand which is to place myself at the beginning of this, what everyone is referring to as the Third Millennium. Oh, I should not say everyone for the Japanese have an entirely different way of counting their years which is to count them from the advent of each new emperor's reign which makes infinitely more sense in that we are always starting over in our multifaceted attempts at living. The Japanese. That seems an honest and logical way to start this memoir for Japan has been a large influence on my life in that some twenty-five years ago I married Etsuko in Tokyo, married her, in fact, three times on the same day.

●

We were riding the train north out of Tokyo to Isesaki to meet Etsuko's parents for the first time. To say I was not looking forward to this would be akin to saying that in general I do not look forward to root canal surgery, a procedure I have endured twice before. Because we had been living together in my Ichikawa apartment for three months as unmarried as one coupling couple can be, and that because they were traditional folk from the country who had told her as a young girl never to marry anyone with blond hair and blue eyes, well, my rather reserved enthusiasm could be understood.

"They'll love you," Etsuko said as we were riding in the back of the taxi cab from Isesaki station.

"Your father, too?"

Etsuko had paused, was looking at the gray that winter had put down on the rice paddies we were passing through on a long and open road, paddies that had once been green and were waiting to be so once again.

"Well?" I pressed.

"Okay," she said, turning to look at me with a tenuous frown of disappointment, now a moue. "You're right. Maybe not him."

"Ha! I knew it. And what about your older brother?"

She turned to look out her window and I could see the reflection of a slight smile. "No, not him. Definitely not him. He loves only himself."

"Okay, what about your sister?"

8

She turned back to me. "We won't see her, but I would have to say that she might love you some if you told her you were Christian."

"Why is that?"

"She'd like an ally. She's the only Christian in the family. The others are Buddhist and Shinto."

"So I should sell my soul to be loved?"

"No. She probably wouldn't love you even if you were Christian."

"So, then," I said. "Only your mother. Only she will love me."

"No, Jake, now that I truly consider this, maybe not even her."

I gave her a long and hard frown until she burst into the laughter that she so often found refuge in, and then I laughed too, but mine was a nervous laugh and hers may have been as well.

We pulled into the yard through the gate, paid the driver and walked up the steps of the front porch. We were deep in the country and after living in Tokyo for three years, the rich fecundity of cow dung, the harried squawk of chickens, and the open space of rice paddies was liberating after the huddled concrete confinement of the city. Etsuko opened the door and said, "*Tadaima.*" We waited for someone to appear, my feeling of liberation now erstwhile and dead in my wake.

•

It is exactly on this last sentence that Etsuko knocks on my office door (I was about to look up the word erstwhile to check both the spelling and the meaning–it is an odd looking word, one that I am not sure I have ever employed in a sentence). She opens it and enters. "How are you feeling?"

"Oh, all right."

She laughs. "Sure. You and Gunnar drank a bottle of Calvados. And after what, four bottles of wine? Sure you feel all right."

"Okay, Etsuko. I feel like an anvil after a hard night of service."

"I remember that." She walks up next to me and looks at my computer monitor. "That was a line from your book, which one, *Road*

9

to the Sea?"

"Yep. I always liked that simile."

"It's funny that you quote yourself."

"My mind is full of echoes."

"Jake Weedsong, you are a funny and unusual man." She kisses me on the cheek.

"Thank you."

"Do you want some lunch? We have leftover lamb."

"I don't think so. Thanks, though."

"Okay. Then I'll see you this evening. I'm going into town." She kisses me on the cheek again and on the way out the door she says, "*Gambatte.*"

"*Gambatte-masu,*" I reply.

I have never found a pure definition for the word, but it means something like hang in there and be tough even though there are five men with long knives dismembering you with careful deliberation. (I should say here how I admire the stolid stoicism of the Japanese, their hard-as-nails demeanor in the face of every Waterloo: Japan is surely the only nation in the world virtually bereft of whiners.)

Etsuko is going to Portland State University where she is a professor of Japanese. It is Wednesday and she teaches in the afternoon, one class today, I think. Sometimes I find myself wondering what her students think of her, if they find her attractive as do I, as did I professors of my own when I was a young student. I remember the Latin professor at the University of Oregon. I do not recall her name, only what we called her: The Fox. And she was that. I must admit that when she stood before the class leading us in the declension of certain nouns, my own mind was occupied in the declension of her clothing from top to bottom so that finally she stood before us *declinatio*, the language of Latin rendered very much alive. It was Lord Byron who wrote, *I love the language, that soft bastard Latin/Which melts like kisses from a female mouth* and it is those lines that I think of when I think of The Fox.

In the sixth century B.C., Lao Tsu wrote that *not seeing desirable things prevents confusion of the heart,* but I must now say that though I read and studied Taoism as a young man, it never alleviated the great and bewildered chaos that boomed beneath my breast. Everything of beauty brought on desire so that in Aristotle's terms I was a firmly informed young man for it was he who said, "Man is his desire" and I was mine.

I, too, taught at Portland State University. I was a professor of creative writing up until two years ago when I was fired for having done nothing more than throw a glass of beer on a student at a social gathering of faculty and graduate students in the creative writing program. Ms. Virginia Frost was a surly young woman who believed that she was God's gift to the world of letters (in fact, her prose, while grammatically sound, had all the profundity of a snow shovel). She was also a self-righteous vegan, one of those narrow-minded people who, so as not to be hypocrites, should only be allowed to eat seeds that have been winnowed from their host plants by the wind. Anyway, she was sitting down with Alex Karmanoff, a student whose poetry I was told by his professor Gunnar Hoagart showed all the promise of a Las Vegas marriage. "Virginia," I said. "But aren't those leather shoes you are wearing?" I do admit I was a tad tipsy, but whenever I wax bibulous, my social restraint wanes accordingly which means I become quite honest.

"So?"

Ah, I thought: this would be a victory (little did I then know of how Pyrrhic in nature). "But Virginia, I thought you were a vegan like your character Elyse in your last story who lived on seeds in a nunnery."

"Professor Weedsong, it was not a nunnery. She lived in a commune."

"But you are a vegan."

"Yes."

"And the leather shoes?"

She positively glared at me. "None of your fucking business, you, you writer *manque.*"

This, of course, was when I tossed the beer on her. I had only

11

meant to splash the contents of my glass into her face, but, alas, the glass slipped from my hand and crashed into her face doing some sweet damage to her nose and cutting her lip quite nicely. She screamed histrionically and I could see the blood seep from between her fingers when she covered her face with her hands. Alex stood up and stared at me with his fists clenched at his sides in her great defense. "Easy, Alex, she's hardly worth fighting over," I said. By now the students had gathered around us as well as the members of the faculty. I had created quite a stir. Alex was busy recounting my transgression in what sounded to me like a close yet strange approximation of spondaic pentameter when Gunnar put his arm around my shoulder and in an effort to alleviate my worries, said quite drunkenly, "Well, old buddy, I guess it's tits up for you around here." Gunnar, Oregon's Poet Laureate, or Poet Lariat as I refer to his position when he has been roped in to reciting verse on solemn political occasions, has always had a way with words.

As I made my way for the exit, I quite proudly and drunkenly repeated, "Who's afraid of Virginia Frost, who's afraid of Virginia Frost," and then I was gone, out in the open air of a September night, wondering what Edward Albee was writing that day.

•

It may seem to the reader that I am without narrative resolve, but that is not the case. I flit back and forth in time here, from country to country, from job to job, for that is indeed how I have lived my life up and down and across the board until now. In short, I have lived without plan. In embarking upon the writing of this memoir, surely as vainglorious an activity as there can be, I thought I would organize it in chronological fashion starting back in Japan, but upon further reflection I realized that the reader would require some knowledge of who was looking back in order to understand how I color and interpret my own past through the lens that has been so affected by all of my undertakings since Etsuko and I moved to the states. In short, my having been dismissed from a teaching position will certainly affect the way I recall meeting Etsuko's parents that gray January day. Besides, memory is largely a product of desire. I remember Ogden Nash writing *How confusing the beams from memory's lamp are;/One day a bachelor, the next a grampa/What is the secret of the trick?/How did I get old so quick?* I also remember him writing *Candy is dandy, but liquor is quicker.* He was a man of simple fun.

I am not a bitter man and that is due in large part to the hefty settlement my lawyer exacted from the university, so hefty, in fact, as to make tenable this agrarian life spent appeasing that greatest of Greek Gods, Dionysus, and I do so with long rows of Pinot noir and Pinot gris grapes that curve their way up and down these fecund hills that ride as shoulders on this green bellied valley in which I live.

●

After Etsuko had announced our presence, we waited. I heard a shuffling gait approach, a susurrus of steps like a carpenter lightly sanding a thin cherry plank, and then Etsuko's mother appeared, draped in a silk kimono, smiling, then laughing, tears running down her cheeks. She had a smile the saddest of worlds could enter, and a large gold tooth that twinkled the doldrums away. Immediately, I knew I loved her with as much assurance as I knew I loved her daughter.

"Mother," Etsuko said in Japanese. "This is Jake Weedsong. Jake, this is my mother."

We both bowed and said that we were pleased to meet each other, and then I bowed again out of respect, and then she, too, bowed again so that we bobbed for a moment like two chickens working at feed.

We removed our shoes, put on house slippers and were led to the living room where we sat down on the tatami mat floor at the *hori gotatsu*, a low table beneath which the floor planks had been removed so that we could sit on the floor with our legs comfortably extended beneath us where a small electric heater warmed the air. Cloth skirts hung from the table's sides covering our laps, and these skirts contained the warm air so that from the waist down we were quite cozy. The room itself was chilly, however, as the only heat source was a kerosene heater that burned in the corner of the room. Estuko and her mother went off into the kitchen and I could hear their muffled talking, and some giggling which I felt was directed at me.

I sat there looking at the room where Etsuko had grown up, trying to imagine it through her eyes. There were two shrines on the wall, one Buddhist and one Shinto, though I could not discern which was which, and there was a scroll with large Kanji characters which I could not read. There were book shelves against one wall, and *shoji*— sliding doors pasted with thin, white paper—were closed to the hallway. The outside wall was interrupted with sliding glass doors through which I could see a gray field and then houses with blue tiled roofs and then, in the distance, dark mountains that climbed into ashen clouds. I wondered what evenings were like when Etsuko was a little girl and she had come home from school and the family was gathered here for dinner. Was it here, at this very *kotatsu*, that her mother had said with a laugh, "Never marry a man with blond hair and blue eyes"? It may well have been and here I was, a once ethereal admonition now manifested solidly whole.

They came back with a tray of cups and a pot of tea and when they sat down and Etsuko's mother poured me a cup of green tea, I said with some hesitation, "*Domo arrigato, okaasan.*" Thank you, *mother.*

If she were taken aback, it was only for an instant for after her jaw dropped revealing a gold flash, she smiled and said I was welcome. And I really felt I was. We sat and drank tea and ate sembei and mikans, and we talked and laughed like laughter were in excessive supply. Then I told her I wanted to marry Etsuko and she laughed again.

"You want to marry Etsuko?"

"Yes, I do."

"But you know she is lazy?"

"Yes, I do."

"Very, very, lazy?"

"The laziest of women around," I said. Etsuko gave both her mother and me mild looks of reprimand, but did not seem displeased.

"She is the laziest girl in all of Japan," her mother said as she poured more tea. "See? I must pour my own tea."

"Yes, the laziest."

Of course, none of this was true, but I now think and thought at the time that one, her mother had never had a gaijin in such close proximity, and two, she had never had anyone, especially a *gaijin*, tell her he wanted to marry her daughter, and the only way to handle such large shocks to the system was to deflect them with a humor that could distract one from the reality at hand. If I thought how difficult this was for me at the time, I did not understand how impossibly complicated this was for her, a woman who had just been called mother by a man with blond hair and blue eyes.

•

I am walking between two rows of Pinot gris with Bacchus, our six year old yellow lab, thinking about Etsuko's mother and what I had written today, when I see Etsuko driving up the gravel road in her Subaru station wagon. The rows are ten feet wide so as to accommodate American gauge tractors, but I would prefer a slightly narrower row. European tractors are available, but if ever a spare part were needed it would be weeks of waiting before it were in my hand. Thus, we keep the rows at ten feet but can still create more density by interplanting shoots into the ground between existing vines. This, we have found, is possible in Oregon because we have phylloxera-free soil here. Unlike in sunny California, here it is necessary to train the plants vertically so as to increase leaf exposure to light, and I have been working on the design of a new trestle constructed like those used for hops, only smaller in stature, of course.

It is on late afternoons like today when I walk through the

vineyard that I do my best creative thinking, whether it be applied to my writing or to the vineyard or to nothing at all (I recall this from Lao Tsu: *Empty yourself of everything. Let the mind rest at peace*). I simply walk without direction, my thoughts running free, interrupted by the occasional pheasant that Bacchus will flush, or by a small covey of quail bursting into oblivion against the luteous wall of dusk. Oh, I think, I should have thrown a beer on a student many years before.

At the house, I find Etsuko unpacking groceries. "How goes it, dear?" I ask as I enter the garage.

"I saw your little nemesis today," she says as she pulls a bag from the back seat.

"Virginia Frost?" I kiss her on the cheek before picking up the last bag of groceries and we walk into the kitchen together, Bacchus just behind. "Did you speak to her?"

"I told her Safeway had prime rib on sale." She sets her bag on the counter as do I.

"You did not." We begin unbagging the groceries, putting them in their proper places.

She laughs. "No, no, I did not."

"How did she look?"

"Lots of cotton but still the leather shoes."

"I figured she would have matriculated by now, but maybe she's just another hanger-on afraid to leave the academic nest for the uncertainties of the big, bad world where the hawks await her flesh and blood."

"And where strange men will throw glasses of beer in her face."

"Touche. Say, what about a beer? Or a glass of wine?"

"A beer for me."

I go to the refrigerator and take out two bottles of the amber ale I had brewed, carefully pour two glasses so as not to kick up any sediment at the bottom of the bottle, and we sit down at the kitchen table. Bacchus comes in from the living room, nuzzles my crotch and lies down at my feet.

"How did the writing go today under the heavy hand of Calvados?" She takes a sip of her beer. "Say, this is a good batch."

"Thanks. Oh, it went fine. I am recounting my meeting your mother who, by the way, I would have married if not for you."

"Or my father."

"True. He, too, was an obstacle. Anyway, the memoir is going fine."

"What does Cindy say?"

Cindy has been my editor at Crayton Books for ten years now. I'm afraid I am her big disappointment for I write fiction of a literary nature without big plots that remind dullards to turn the pages in order to come to the end. I am her mid-list failure, sad to say. "Oh, Cindy doesn't think too highly of a book that doesn't have any special effects. I told her I was writing about a man and a woman's life together."

"And what did she say to that?"

"She dismissed me and the book by saying I was a writer's writer."

"That seems to me a compliment, Jake."

"Yes, maybe, though unintentional. And how are things at the university?"

"Fine."

"Aren't you getting tired of the drudgery of it all? You don't have to keep working."

"I still enjoy it. Anyway, I'm up for sabbatical in a year."

"I never really asked you this, Etsuko, but weren't you angry at me that I got fired?"

She laughs. I love Etsuko in so many ways, and her laughter reminds me of how lucky I am. "At least you threw the beer at a deserving target. The little bitch." She laughs again. "But I must say, you do seem more content now."

"It's funny, but I am. Writing was all I ever wanted, but I had to teach, of course, or do something to make money. Sometimes I wonder what I could have written had I been able to devote each day to it. You know, today I took my time over each sentence, each word, but I never had that luxury before. And then I walked through the vineyard thinking about the words I had strung together. A couple of years ago I would have been reading student papers. That's how I learned to misspell the simplest of words."

"I'm glad for you, Jake."

I reach across the table and take her hand in mine. "I love you, Etsuko." I stand up and lean to her and kiss her on the lips. Bacchus gets up and barks, her otter tail swinging back and forth off my leg. She is of a jealous nature.

I sit back down. Etsuko says, "Jake, I love you, too. Now tell me, what is it you are cooking for dinner."

"Veal Marsala with which we will have a '98 Pinot noir."

"Okay, then. I'll go grade these papers. Call me when dinner is ready."

She gets up to go. "I'll call you with bells on," I say. Then I stand and go to the cupboard and put on an apron, thinking what magic there is in life when two people can love each other as do we. If we were geese and a hunter shot her, I would fly right into the barrel of his gun.

•

Everything was going smoothly, swimmingly as I've heard the English say, when we heard the front door open, and Etsuko's mother got up from the *kotatsu* and went to greet her son. My anxiety at meeting more members of my new family was palpable enough to cause Etsuko to say, "Relax, Jake. He's just my older brother." Of course, this did nothing to appease my wild nerves.

"What is his name again?"

"Tsuyoshi."

"Tsuyoshi," I repeated soon after which I heard a booming voice from the hallway say, "Tsuyoshi-SAN." If things had been going swimmingly before, I now felt both lungs fill with water, my body sinking to the briny depths.

"He can be an asshole," Etsuko said in English.

"I forgot the honorific. I will say he has good ears."

And then he appeared in the room, standing tall above us, a chiseled face that might never have borne a smile. I stood and instinctively reached out my hand though I knew better. He backed away a good two feet and gave a little nod of the head as if his tie were too tight, then turned on his heel and went into the kitchen leaving me standing there with my arm outstretched. I pulled my arm back and sat back down. "I don't think he likes me."

By now, Etsuko was up and in the kitchen and I heard her talking to her brother in a harsh and unfriendly tone, and then her mother, too, took on the universal tone of a mother disappointed in a grown child. Soon after, he left through the front door and Etsuko rejoined me as I sat worried about all the turmoil I had caused, rather, that love had caused along with my blond hair and blue eyes.

"Don't worry, Jake. He can be a pig."

"I shouldn't have stuck out my hand. It was just an instinct. I know well enough to bow. It just happened."

"He could have shaken your hand, Jake."

"And I should have bowed."

"But you didn't mean to."

"I know. But I must try to understand it from his point of view. I insulted him."

"He could have been more gracious."

Then her mother came in, my own future mother, and I said in Japanese, "*Okaasan, gomennasai. Watashi-wa machigai desu.*" Both women laughed until tears rolled down their cheeks. What I had meant to say, of course, was *Mother, I am sorry. I made a mistake.* But what I literally said, as Etsuko explained, was *Mother, I am sorry. I am a mistake.*

Etsuko said that her older brother would agree with my self-assessment whole heartedly, and then she laughed again.

●

Bacchus woke me this morning She knows not to do this, but the wind was blowing hard and she is frightened of the wind. She lay on the floor on my side of the bed and I woke to her muffled whimpering. I knew that the only reason she made this pitiful sound was to wake me for as soon as I leaned over the edge of the bed to look down on her, she stopped her mournful cry, the very energy of the whimpering moving from her mouth and back through her body and into her tail which now swished back and forth. "God damn it, Bacchus," I said. "It's just the wind, for Christ's sake." She positively smiled at the sound of my voice, and then she stood, her hips swinging back and forth in conflict with the pivot of her tail so that it appeared that she was trying to undress from her own skin. I knew it was no good now, so I stood and she followed me to the kitchen where I started a pot of coffee.

That was four hours ago and now it is almost nine in the morning. Etsuko left for the university an hour ago, and I have been sitting here writing since she left. Every morning before I write, I read what I have written the day before, and I am finding it quite enjoyable to relive that frightening day when I met Etsuko's family. I realize now that her brother was merely fulfilling his duties as the oldest brother for he was worried that I was surely a foreigner from afar temporarily living with his younger sister, for after we were married he showered me with gifts and we became if not friends then relatives who could laugh and drink together in holiday toleration.

Today is our daughter Elin's birthday. She is twenty-one today. I miss her terribly for she and I have always been so close as to know each other's thoughts even before we know them ourselves. When she was born, I stayed home for a year taking care of her as Etsuko worked at the university, and on cold winter days when she was just six months old, I would bundle her up, put her in the back pack, and fish the banks of the Wilson River for the big winter steelhead that had made the journey home to spawn. I believe that these early outdoor activities were what partly formed her into the athletic Tom Boy she has always been. The Nature or Nurture argument is just one large false dilemma for it is certainly a bit of Nature and a bit of Nurture that forms us into who we are, and those who believe we are solely hard-wired to be who we are should stick the barrel of a large gun in their mouths and squeeze the trigger for there is no reason for them to live, for if the game is predetermined, why play? Anyway, Elin played every sport growing up, and by age fourteen was such a good wing-shot that weak men would not hunt with us for fear of being shown up. I will say she often showed me up, once even shooting triple quail as I missed two, and I was so proud of being out-shot that I blushed through an inch of skin.

Elin is a senior at Stanford riding out a scholarship as point guard of their basketball team and playing catcher and batting fourth on the softball team that won the national championship last year, and should do so once again. She is studying sociology because, she says, she likes everything in life so much that she wants to do it all and sociology, she explains, encompasses entirety. I asked her what she plans to do with such a degree, and then she asked me what I had planned on doing with a degree in English, and that was the logical end of that discussion.

Etsuko and I had wanted to fly down to Palo Alto tonight, but the team is in North Carolina playing Duke so we will have to celebrate her birthday by watching her on t.v. Whenever we watch Elin play on t.v., Etsuko wears earplugs as she says that I become loud and out of control in my directives to the referees. After one of what I thought was one of my most creative outbursts, Etsuko said, "Jake, that is biologically impossible so please be quiet." Anyway, tonight we will watch the game and then as we lie in bed, I will replay the entire game in my head, choreographing each of Elin's acrobatic moves, missing her dearly.

When Elin was eleven, I wanted to freeze time forever. It was a wonderful age. Elin went to a Montessori school and was as happy a child as there ever were. Maria Montessori, by the way, was an absolute genius and if she were alive today she would be appalled in seeing how this country goes about educating its youth. Everyone whines about crime and rallies to build more prisons, but there is rarely more than a murmur addressing the need to improve education. In fact, many of these dual income families today who never share a meal together blame the teachers themselves when they should pony up to the mirror and confess to having never taken their children to a baseball game where they could teach their children how to score the game and how to figure batting averages, much more valuable skills than knowing how to program a VCR.

During my last year at the university, the deans were all making a big push for Distance Learning, a curious oxymoron in and of itself. It was a dollar-and-cents decision on their part as it was to cut English composition as a requirement for Freshmen. They even asked me to teach a creative writing class on-line to students living around the state of Oregon, but I refused, saying that I believed in the dynamics of a classroom filled with warm bodies where I could look in the students' eyes and see the manifestation of learning. One of the greatest virtues of the Humanities is that people can sit together and discuss the literature that bonds us all and to attempt to do so through cyber spatial chat rooms is ironic at best. As the computer creeps into every facet of our lives to the extent that we will never have to leave our homes unless we want to, we become more and more dehumanized. If I were a writer of portentous science fiction, I would now write a story of a world where there is no urban core; rather, I would describe a world of warehouses from which people would order their daily needs via the internet. No more talks with your favorite grocer, just type in agoraphobia dot com.

●

We sat and drank tea throughout the afternoon, and as the blue of the winter day fell into the maws of dusk, my nerves rallied in anticipation of the impending return home of father. Frankly, I was tiring of all this green tea and was longing for something bibulous to bolster my spirits, but Etsuko told me that her parents rarely drank alcohol.

Finally, the front door opened and I heard a deep male voice say "*Tadaima*," as mother scrambled up and left us with a nervous smile. Both Etsuko and I stood, and I reminded myself not to attempt to shake his hand, but to bow deeply at the waist instead.

When father entered the sitting room where we had spent the entire afternoon, he first looked at his daughter and then at me.

"*Konbanwa, Otosan*," she said as she bowed.   Good evening, father.

"*Konbanwa, Otosan*," I said as I bowed, and when I looked up, he gave me a short bow in return, but he wore a look of numbed surprise and it may have been because I had called him father.

As Etsuko and her mother cooked in the kitchen, I sat across the table from her father who had the newspaper unfurled so that I could not see his face. Finally, I got up and went to the kitchen and told Etsuko that I was going for a short walk in the neighborhood for I was in need of some physical activity after sitting down all afternoon.

Etsuko told her mother of my plan, and she stopped chopping onions and said something to Etsuko that I did not understand. "Jake, you cannot go for a walk," Etsuko said as she rolled out some sushi.

"What? Just a short one. I'll be back for dinner."

She turned to look at me. "No, Jake. My mother doesn't want you to be seen by the neighbors."

"What?"

"They haven't been told that I am living with a *gaijin*."

"Oh."

"You have to remember that many of the older people out here in the country have never met a Caucasian. You could cause a heart attack." Etsuko smiled and then I did, too, for though I was a little miffed about the house arrest, I also understood that Etsuko's family had been living on this land for hundreds of years as had the neighboring families and my pride would have to be kept on a short leash for it was I who was the encroacher here and it would serve me best to remember that.

Still, I had a card to play. "I understand completely," I told Etsuko. Her mother was cutting onions and her eyes were welled up with tears. In Japanese I said, "I love you," and then I locked on to Etsuko's lips for a long and passionate kiss and embrace.

Then I turned to mother whose jaw was unhinged, and I told her she was beautiful and that I loved her, too, and I gave her a short kiss on the cheek. Both women blushed, and I left them there, scarlet cheeked, the mother and her daughter whom I would marry for my wife.

●

Etsuko's mother and father are coming to visit next week. Etsuko is nervous about this, but excited as well. They'll stay here for one month. I imagine they are quite nervous themselves for neither has been outside of Japan and to have lived seventy some years before one's first trip abroad certainly must corrupt one's expectations.

I hear the doorbell ring and remember that Gunnar is coming out today with an advance copy of his new poetry collection. I get up, walk down the hall and find Bacchus standing by the door wagging her tail. Labs do not make good guard dogs and would only delay a burglary with their tongues and drool to slip on.

"Gunnar," I say as I open the door and wait for the inevitable hug. Gunnar grew up in California and is a hugger, something I have never been. I was born and reared here in Oregon, and it has always amused me to see Oregonians proclaim themselves natives of this state with bumper stickers that read Native Oregonian when the true natives have been relegated to barren reservations where the only crop that can be grown is the casino. Besides, to strut like a peacock because your mother birthed you on a particular slab of land seems a rather bird-brained activity. Oregonians are provincial which is so often true of those in incestuous climes and the influx of Californians can only be seen as revitalizing what has been a stagnant and murky gene pool. Still, I could do without the hugging.

After extricating myself from his powerful embrace (Gunnar is a large and hardy man of some two-hundred-twenty pounds wrought onto his six foot-two inch frame), he hands me the new book which is entitled *Dusk at Sunrise*. We walk down the hall, he following me, me admiring the cover on which is a photograph of the sun setting behind my vineyard hill. "Shit, Gunnar, it's absolutely beautiful."

"It is, isn't it? The photo came out quite well."

"It's beautiful," I say, still staring at the picture. "How about a glass of wine to celebrate? I've got a new Muller-Thurgau chilled."

Gunnar looks at his watch. "What the hell. It's after nine."

We go to the kitchen where I open the bottle and pour two glasses. We stand by the window and we clink glasses. "To the maestro of the stanza and to great success with the new book. Cheers."

We each drink. I take the bottle and we walk back to the living room where the front windows look out upon the rolling hills of this vineyard which stands at the foot of the Coast Range. It is another gray January day with the deep green of the distant Douglas Firs striking black against the sunless clouds. We sit down on the sofa where we can look out over the vineyard. "How are things in the hallowed halls?"

"Oh, the same as ever. Say, this is a good wine."

"The good doctor Hermann Muller-Thurgau came up with a winner when he crossed the Riesling and Silvaner vines."

"We might play with some crossbreeds."

"We could, Gunnar."

"How's the writing?"

"It's going well. Having my mornings freed up these past two years has been great. You ought to throw a beverage in a student's face."

Gunnar laughs. "I still think about that evening from time to time. God, but was that funny."

"Etsuko says she saw our Ms. Frost yesterday."

"She's still around. She's gone to wearing all black now, including a beret."

"She must be switching genres, the poor girl. From prose to verse. Well, you can have her."

"She won't take classes from me because of my association with you, I fear."

"That's the biggest favor anyone could do for you."

"It's certainly worth a lunch."

"A lunch? Are you kidding me? My keeping her out of your classes is worth a thundering herd of Kobe beef and a rambunctious school of *fugu*."

"A big lunch then. Say, how about a little more of that wine." He reaches for the bottle on the glass coffee table before us and pours first me and then himself another glass. After a sip, he says, "Did you eat blowfish in Japan?"

"Yeah, once. This wealthy friend of Etsuko's took us out to a fancy *fugu* restaurant in Tokyo. We were the only customers. We sat around a *kotatsu*, the three of us, eating and drinking sake for three or four hours. The chef would cook each part of the fugu a different way and it would be served separately."

"It's true that the *fugu* chefs have to be licensed?"

"Hell, yes. Every year a handful of people die in Japan from eating *fugu* that was not properly prepared. Poison-tainted somehow during the preparation. Tetrotoxin. Apparently most of it is in the ovaries and the liver. The ovaries were incredible. When you eat them, they numb your tongue."

"It was good?"

"The best fish I have ever had in my life. And I don't know if it was because I ate knowing full well it could have been the last fish I ever ate in my life. Eating dinner that night was like playing Russian Roulette."

Gunnar set his glass down. "Except with a purpose. You weren't risking your life for nothing. I mean, you were eating something absolutely exotic."

"True. The fish is white and they cut it so thin that when it is laid out on the plates, you can see the colorful designs of the plate right through the fish."

"Would you do it again?"

I thought about this for a moment before replying. I took a sip of wine. The reason conversations are so often banal, I think, is precisely because people feel the necessity to respond so quickly without truly thinking about what they are about to say. "I don't think so. If I did, it would necessarily dilute the strength of that first experience, and then I would have less of a story to tell, less of a memory to savor. But eating a good food that can kill you is certainly more rewarding than eating something safe but insipid."

"We're most alive when we are closest to death."

"You are waxing ironic, Gunnar. Maybe you should have called the book *Sunrise at Dusk*. Is that, do you suppose, a product of aging, this recognition of life's ironies?"

"It's too early in the morning for me to say, Jake, and I have not had near enough of the wine." He stands up now. "Anyway, I've brought you the book. I hope you find it worthy of a good review."

I stand as well. "Oh, I am sure it will be every bit as good as all your other books. Besides, I've already read all the poems. They're quite good."

We walk to the front door. I open it and he walks out into the brisk, wet air of an Oregon January. "Well, thanks for taking the time to write the review, Jake. And thanks for the wine."

"My pleasure. Remember, we're having dinner on Friday."

After Gunnar leaves, I go back to my study, lie down on the couch and begin reading the poems of Gunnar Hoagart as collected in *Dusk at Sunrise*, the irony of a poet in his waning years.

Last night Etsuko and I watched as Stanford beat Duke in overtime. Elin played well, scoring nine points and dishing out eleven

27

assists. When Elin hit a three-pointer to tie the game with a minute left in regulation, my eyes welled and tears dribbled down my cheeks. Etsuko put her arm around my shoulders and hugged me, not once removing her stare at the television screen.

I am convinced that happiness and sadness are so inextricably related and that they each can be enjoyed. Seeing my daughter play basketball on television took me back to when I coached her team when she was a little girl, and this made me both happy and sad, happy for the memory and sad that it is only that. I cry with absolute equanimity at things both woebegone and blithe.

Etsuko is still asleep. I started my morning with a dark walk around the vineyards with Bacchus in the lead, her head to the ground as she snorted away every scent before us leaving the earth bereft of redolence, the hanging quarter moon looking as if it were about to tip and roll over until it would fall out of the sky and into the day. Bacchus flushed a covey of quail which spooked me, their fluttered wings tearing out the black wall of the false dawn. Then, with the morning opened, I went to my study and began to work.

•

My matrimonial history is surely rare in that I have been married three times without losing a spouse to divorce or death, married three times to the same woman on the same day. Two months before the wedding, we did our reconnaissance for a suitable locale for Marriage Number Three which would logically follow marriages numbers one and two. Marriage Number One was to be held at the *Shiyakusho,* city hall, and Marriage Number Two would follow at the American embassy in Tokyo's Toranomon district. These two marriages would appease the respective governments under whose politics Etsuko and I were respectively born. Why we had to appease two nations is absolutely beyond my ken, however. That each national government demanded our fealty as if we were mere vassals and they the lords renders my stomach so sour as to cause the bile to rise. But what was there to do?

At the city hall, we filled out the necessary paper work and were essentially married in the eyes of the Japanese government, and then we went to the American embassy where we had started the paper work some four months earlier.

The Americans had demanded police records from China where Etsuko had lived for two years as a graduate student at Beijing University. These American diplomats in Tokyo feared that I could be marrying a communist, and they demanded that Etsuko sign an affidavit saying she was not a member of the Communist Party. If I did not realize it before, it certainly became apparent to me then that the American government had my best interests under consideration because all my love for Etsuko, that elusive eros, would have to be withdrawn and deposited with someone else if it were discovered that this young woman were a communist who was bent on marrying me so as to infiltrate American intelligence through the subterfuge of marriage so as to gain access to our secrets in teaching English: *Ah ha, your prepositions indicate both space and time. Wait until my leaders learn of this: we will know just where and when to drop the bomb.*

Our third marriage of the day was to be the unifying celebration of our love.

Some three months before, I had visited a Lutheran church in the Iidabashi District of Tokyo. The pastor, John Carlson, was a Minnesotan who had lived in Tokyo some twenty years with his wife and his children who attended the American School in Shibuya. He was a large man with pot roast hands and he sat behind his desk in apparent discomfort at being confined in a chair when he should have been walking through open dairy land with the breeze messing his long blond hair.

"So, you are getting married? And you would like to do so here in our church?" He had a note pad open before him and a pen stuck in his hand like a flag pole atop a mountain.

"Yes." I sat across the desk from him, and I was nervous for some unknown reason. In retrospect, it was my agnosticism that caused my anxiety.

"Are you Lutheran?"

"No. I mean, I was. But not now. No longer. I mean, I don't believe in all that anymore."

"You mean you don't believe in God?" He leaned forward, his hands atop the desk now as if he were ready to push off and pounce on the apostate that I was.

"Yes, that's right. Yes, I don't believe." I found myself blushing.

He leaned back in his chair and sighed. He did not seem happy with me. "Why not?"

"Why don't I believe?"

"Yes, why don't you believe?"

"Hmm." I thought a moment. It was, after all, a good question. It wasn't that I did not want to believe. In fact, I wanted to believe. It would make him happier and it would make me happier. That's what religion did: it whitewashed all the tough questions so that we could carry on our lives without unanswerable questions constantly pestering us so that we could ignore the diaphanous yet stentorian chorus of *You Don't Know, You Don't Know. Ha, Ha, Ha. You Don't Know. Na, na, na na na, You doooon't know, Oo*.

"Well?"

"I don't know."

"What?"

"Because it doesn't make sense?"

"What?"

"God? Heaven. Hell. All that. Jesus on the cross. Rising from the dead. The trinity. A virgin giving birth. None of it makes an ounce of sense to me. Though I like the water into wine."

"Then why come here to see if you can get married in the church?"

"Because it is a nice building and it is centrally located. How much, by the way, for the service?"

"I don't know."

I could see he was hurt by my candor. "Look, I'm sorry. It just seems a logical place to get married. It is, after all, a beautiful building."

He was leaning back in his chair now. "You were raised as a Lutheran?"

"Yes, I was. In Portland, Oregon."

"What happened?"

"You really want to know?"

"Yes."

"Well, for one thing, church was so depressing. All those bleak songs. *Amazing Grace! How sweet the sound that saved a wretch like me.* I mean, no one had called me a wretch anywhere else but in church. And the stained glass. I hated the stained glass. Pictures of this guy hanging from a cross, naked, and his face held the most woeful expression I've ever seen, head atilt, jaw hanging down, nails through his hands, arms and legs. Bleak as hell. Imagine a six year old looking at those pictures and then listening to those sad songs. Bleak. It was bleak. And my parents made me go."

"They were instructing you." He crossed his arms and leaned back in his chair.

"Yeah, I suppose. But they never questioned the church, either. When I was fifteen, I told them that's it, I'm done, through, I'm not going anymore."

"And?"

"And what? There was nothing they could do." I paused for a moment. Carlson was not looking very pleased at any of this. "Say, tell me something. Do you really believe in hell?"

"Of course." He clenched his jaw and pursed his lips in confident confirmation.

"And do you really believe that those of us who do not accept Jesus Christ as our personal savior, do you really believe we will go to hell?" I leaned forward in my chair, he leaned back in his, and it occurred to me then that maybe he thought I was the devil arrived in

Tokyo to tempt him to some terrible undertaking like maybe going to the sex shows in Shinjuku. (I had heard about them, seen the barkers on the sidewalk, heard about the darkened rooms, the stage with its diaphanous curtains, the girls themselves sensually underclothed, the, wait, I am interrupting the narration of my receiving counsel from a pastor.)

"Yes."

"So, following that logic, if a serial killer who raped and then brutally murdered three women, if he were to repent and accept Christ as his savior, then he would be allowed into heaven?"

"Yes."

"And a humble philanthropist who did nothing but good in his life, a pagan who did not believe Jesus was his savior, this man who volunteered in homeless shelters and who gave much of his income to charity, this man who never hurt another human being, he would be relegated to hell?"

He was quiet now. He said nothing. He was thinking, but about what I was not sure. It seemed that he was thinking what an unfortunate morning it was to have me arrive in his office and to have to carry on a theological discussion so early in the day when he could have been doing crosswords, playing darts?

"Well?" I pressed.

"Well, yes, I would say that, yes, the doctrine, well, he would be, he would end up in hell."

"Okay. Now, how much for the service?"

"Three-hundred thousand yen."

●

As I sit here in my office and write of that day so spatially and temporally removed, I feel sympathy for John Carlson, good man that he was. It was not my intention to question him like that, but it happened just the same. I certainly did not, nor do I want, to appear holier than thou.

It was just a simple fact: I did not believe, nor do I today. And if I am wrong? So be it. I will end up in a hell full of both miscreants and charitable souls. To that, I will have already been acclimated as have us all.

It is Friday morning and Etsuko is at the university. Gunnar and his wife Karla are coming over for dinner this evening and I am to cook a *cassoulet le bouchon*, a perfect dish for this cold and wet January day when the sky falls so low as to render us all on a walk through the heavens bumping our heads on the feet of angels.

I remember going back to see Carlson with Etsuko after he had agreed to perform the service with his Japanese counterpart so that it would be a bilingual ceremony. He had written out a script, so to speak, and we were to practice our parts. When Etsuko read, "And I promise to obey my husband," she put the papers on the desk and said, "I will do no such thing."

Carlson had leaned back in his chair and sighed. Etsuko said that she could not obey me because I was sometimes wrong, and besides, she said, she was not a dog, and now, as I sit here contemplating these historic events, I smile and think of all the mistakes we have avoided because Etsuko *refused* to obey my lead.

"Well, enough for today," I say to Bacchus who lies at my feet. I turn off the computer and stand and Bacchus does, too. Her tail is swinging as if she expects some treat. Often I reflect on the nature of dogs and wish we were more like them. Lao Tsu wrote, *A truly good man is not aware of his goodness, And is therefore good*. With this in mind, I cannot think of a truly good man, not one, but I can think of thousands of good dogs including this Labrador Retriever who waddles at my feet. Surely Lao Tsu knew he was being good some 2500 years ago when he was riding off into the desert to die, disgusted with the ways of men and a gatekeeper persuaded him to write down his teachings for posterity. Surely?

I drive to the Safeway where I make the purchases for tonight's dinner. I know the butcher there, Dave, and am always pleased to see him for he is an artist who truly cares about what he does. It is as if he follows the way of Lao Tsu in that he is accepting of what lies before him without wishing it to be other than it is, and with this understanding he treats everyone with equanimity.

I have lived in Europe and in Africa and in Asia, and I always enjoyed shopping for food on those continents because of the human contact required in the various shops. But in these United States shopping for food, that which sustains us, is antiseptic at best. At least I can have human contact with Dave, however, as we converse about various cuts of meat. I tell him of my recent goose hunt with Gunnar. Dave stands on the other side of the meat counter from me and is dressed in his white apron upon which are smears of blood so that he could be a pallette of just one color. It occurs to me that Virginia Frost could write a bad poem about his garb: *Oh, you breaker of bones/you destroyer of the natural world/ you, you bad, bad butcher, you...*

"You know why geese fly in a Vee, Jake?"

"It's aerodynamically sound. The birds in the back are blocked from the draft." I pick up a package of smoked ham shanks.

"The ham hocks are better." He reaches over and picks up a package and hands it to me at the same time taking the ham shanks from me. "More meat. You know the geese switch positions after resting..."

"Yeah."

"...but do you know why one arm of the Vee is longer than the other?"

I think about this a moment. "No, Dave, I don't."

"Because there are more geese in it."

I mull this over until I see the smile break on Dave's face, and then I laugh, and I am glad that I know this man, this butcher, who can make shopping for meat a true joy.

●

In Japan, Etsuko and I lived in a second story apartment on a small alley next to Tekona shrine, and in the evenings a high, piercing whistle would alert us to the presence of the tofu lady who rode through the neighborhood on her little motorbike selling fresh tofu from a tray that dangled and swung precariously on the back of the bike. The first time I went out to buy some, it was dark and she could not see my face well, but when she heard my American accent, she was for a moment startled before recovering. Then she said, "*Ah, gaijin-san.*" Ah, a foreigner. And for the next two years we had pleasant conversations several evenings each week, and they became as much the period that marked the end of my day as was the chanting of the monks in the morning the colon that everything else followed.

Daimon Doori, Big Gate Street, was a serpentine stretch of about a kilometer between Ichikawa Station where I caught the train weekday mornings and a large gate which served as the entry to Mama-san, a temple on the hill above our apartment. The street, often so narrow that you could simultaneously touch buildings on either side if you stood in the middle and really stretched, housed little bars and restaurants and sundry shops, and it was here that I visited the green grocer and the butcher and the bakery and the liquor store. Shopping at these various merchants, getting to know each one as an individual, grounded me in the reality of living in Japan. I ate and drank what I purchased from these men and women so that their image was always with me. When I ordered a case of beer at the liquor store, twenty one-liter bottles of Sapporo in a plastic crate, the proprietor would deliver it on the back of his motorcycle and the two bottles that were chilled would have ribbons tied on them to identify them as ready for consumption.

My best man, Pat Scott, arrived three weeks before the wedding. I have known Pat all of my life as we grew up across the street from each other. In December, I wrote him and asked him to come to Japan to be my best man, and when he wrote back that he would be there, I was somewhat surprised for Pat had never been out of the United States. In fact, I am not sure whether he had ever been out of Oregon, domestic homebody that he was.

He got a month off from his construction job and arrived in

early May. As I was busy teaching during the day, he was off on his own exploring Tokyo. It was, as he has told me many times since, a life-changing experience for him.

My creative writing students often ask me for one piece of advice that would help their writing, and I tell them: travel. Go places you have never been, I say, even if those places are in the city in which you live. The point is you must go somewhere else to truly see where you have been, and to know that is to begin to know who you are. Without such knowledge, how could one write?

My parents and brother and sister and uncle and aunt and grandfather came to Tokyo for the wedding as did Etsuko's family, and the church filled with our numerous friends who lived in Tokyo, many of whom were Americans I played basketball with on a team called the *Yabanjin*–the hairy barbarians–and teachers with whom I worked.

It was a hot and humid day in May, and I perspired as my brother straightened my tie before I was to walk out before the congregation and wait for Etsuko's father to walk her down the aisle. I stood there, sweat dripping off my chin, and watched as the beautiful Etsuko came down the aisle in measured steps, a full smile spread wide. Her father walked in the bearing of a man with a military history, and his visage bore the mark of dignified severity. I stood wondering exactly what he thought.

I looked at my relatives and then at my future mother-in-law, and she looked sad at losing a daughter, yet happy that we were in love. What must it be like, I wondered, to lose a daughter to a man and his far away place? To have the most unexpected course of events come to pass wherein your daughter, raised on a farm in Gumma, Japan, marries an American from across the sea? It must be something akin to the fruition of melancholy sown by someone else's hand, something that you must harvest and then digest alone.

After Pastor John Carlson had pronounced us man and wife, his Japanese counterpart, Pastor Hideki Kobayashi, gave a speech in Japanese, much of which I did not understand.

Etsuko and I stood before him, our backs to the congregation, and I could feel the perspiration on my forehead. In English, he said, "Jake Weedsong, you come from the United States and are here in Japan having just married Etsuko Suzuki who is from Japan. Thus, you see that though you both speak English, the words you use come from backgrounds thousands of miles apart, and sometimes there will be echoes from each of your homelands that are so faint that you will have to strain to hear them.

"And hear them you must for if you are to understand each other, you must understand the different cultural connotation each word wears over its denotation. In short, you must both work at understanding more than the words can convey. You must understand each other by employing a cultural sensitivity and empathy that goes beyond your two countries' borders. You must understand each other's greatest hopes and greatest fears and with this empathy, Jake, Etsuko, you will become each other and thus you will become one."

At this point, he smiled and said, "Jake Weedsong, you may kiss the bride."

I took Etsuko in my arms and pressed my lips against hers and we kissed a long and passionate kiss. Out of my left eye, I looked into the first pew where I saw Etsuko's mother. As we kissed, I winked at her and she blushed more deeply than September tomatoes.

•

(At this point in the narrative, I find I must confess something to the reader for we are in collaboration here and to conceal my true feelings as I lay these words upon paper is a form of betrayal. Thus, let me say that I have a greater fear of failing in writing this story than I have ever had before, and as each word is laid down, one by one by one, I am host to the dread of having laid them all out for you without having shared any meaningful aspect of our human condition. I only hope you can share my fear for in so doing you will have been me and will have at least shared my angst, as true a part of an honest memoir as can be.)

37

After I return home from the store, and after I put the groceries away, I make myself a *croque madame*, an opened faced broiled ham and cheese sandwich with a fried egg on top, with which I drink a glass of Pinot gris. Bacchus lies at my feet looking up at me through the tops of her brown eyes, that pathetic look labs put on to curry favor. It is that oh, look at poor me, *I've not had a belly rub or a walk or a bone or anything good at all* look that labs are so damned good at feigning. They are pure pathetic.

"Okay, Bacchus," I say, and she immediately sits up and begins the tail wag that polishes our tiled floors, "we'll take a short walk. But I've got to get back to cooking." When she hears the word walk, she erupts with three loud and guttural barks of such fine resonance as to cause the kitchen windows to shudder. In the garage, I put on my shoes, and this causes Bacchus to recommence barking as she watches me lace them up for we do not wear outdoor shoes in the house and she knows that my putting them on more often than not means a walk through open fields.

It is cold out, and I button my red Pendleton jacket to my neck. As we walk down the gravel path toward the pond, Bacchus zigs and zags, her nose to the ground, snorting wildly. I walk behind her, my hands clasped behind my back. The clouds are high today, but there is no rain. This little valley in which I have twenty acres of grapes draped along the rolling hills is five miles outside of the town of Banks, and as I walk, I see the hills rise above me for 360 degrees so it is that I am safely ensconced from the rest of the world, from its dangers of the meanest of ignorant men.

There is something inherently medicinal in a walk with a dog in the country when no leash is required. The dog is free to be her and you are free to be you, yet there is an inextricable connection between the two of you, so that you become part dog running on four paws, tail aflutter. With each step, you fall into a trance until you are no longer consciously thinking and it could well be that you are now a dog and such canine meditation can only be good for you who have for too long thought about money. One can only hope that the dog does not become part you thinking about money and money and money for it seems everything human is fettered to legal tender, oh, leave the dogs unleashed. *Radix malorum est cupiditas*: The Love of money is the root of all evil.

As Bacchus arrives at the pond at the bottom of the hill, six mallards burst into flight, wings transforming air into sound, followed by a pair of wood ducks resplendent in all their color. I stand and look at the water as Bacchus cracks through the thin sheen of ice that extends two or three feet from shore. I could be a dog now, just staring into the water, completely lost in the canine world until Bacchus romps out of the pond. She runs up to me, slams on the brakes with forelegs lowered, and then she shakes the water off her and onto me. Over the years, I have noted that a wet dog must find her guardian before she can shake off. I imagine that if the dog is alone without human companionship that she is content to stay wet, but when a human is in the vicinity, the dog must show off by shaking off every droplet of water in close proximity to the man. Or maybe it is just that they want to share what has been such true pleasure for them? I would like to think that.

We head back up to the house. Bacchus is reluctant to return, but after several whistles she has left the pond and overtaken me on the gravel path, and when we arrive in the garage, I take two bottles of the amber ale from the fridge I keep in the garage. I pour hers in her dish and she immediately laps it up as I take mine in five or six gulps. When she was but three months old and we were living in Portland, we had Gunnar and Karla over for a barbecue. Gunnar was leaning back in a chaise longue and had set his Scotch down on the patio, and Bacchus immediately ran up, stuck her snout into the glass, took a sip, pulled her head out, cocked it first at one angle and then another and coughed. Then she stuck her snout back in and started lapping before Gunnar retrieved the glass and said, "I've seen your kind before."

There are those zealots out there who belong to groups like PETA who would certainly condemn my treating Bacchus to a daily beer, but such thinking is beyond my ken: at six canine years, Bacchus is somewhere around 42 in human years, and if she can't have a beer a day at that age, then, by God, what can she have? Besides, she loves it, and I believe it to be good for her coat and her temperament, though it causes the occasional dyspepsia with its concomitant flatulence.

When Gunnar and I were goose hunting out on Grand Island Sunday last, something disconcerting happened although it made no truck with Bacchus, I suppose. An hour after I had shot my goose, Gunnar shot one and it fell into the pond with a huge splash. Bacchus was in the air leaping into the water before the ringing of my ears abated, and as I looked out on the water I could see that the goose was only winged and now it swam towards the far shore as Bacchus swam after it. Just as Bacchus lowered her head to take the goose in her jaws, the goose dove beneath the surface and disappeared leaving Bacchus momentarily confused as she turned her head every which way in search of the magical goose.

It couldn't have been more than five or six seconds later that the goose popped up above the surface *exactly* behind Bacchus who turned and in seeing her, plunged at it only to have it dive beneath the water once again, and five or six seconds later it resurfaced again *exactly* behind the dog. This went on for five or ten minutes until we realized that Bacchus, now dizzy, was not going to win this battle of wits, so we called her off and had to shoot the goose again. This was upsetting for each of us, of course, and it reminded me that to kill an animal or a fish or a bird is no small act; rather, it is an act of huge consequence and it should be carried out with the dignity the animal deserves. Hunting is a sacred act, and hunters who do not respect the grace of their prey might, quite frankly, be better off shot and killed themselves. Believe me, I have seen these men (and they are inordinately men; women, it seems to me, have more sense and compassion and dignity than do men, and this may be because of their capacity to bear children, but whatever the cause, if we are to be good stewards of this earth, let a woman be in charge). These macho men in their muscle shirts leave Portland and head east of the Cascades to their elk camp and a week later they drive back having made damn sure that the kill is visible in the back of the truck to all who pass. Some of them even cut off the elk's head and tie it down on the hood of their trucks giving all of us hunters a bad rap. Many of these men are uneducable and I would not shed any tears if they were killed. I felt more remorse at watching that arm of geese fly back over Gunnar and me after I shot down one of their own than I would feel over the death of one of these Neanderthals whose hunting rights should be forever suspended.

Cassoulet le Bouchon is a stew favored in Southwestern France in the cold and wet winter months, and it is the perfect dish for today for as I pour a pound of pre-soaked Great Northern beans into two and a half quarts of water, I look out the window and see it is raining now and the sky is gray and sinking as the afternoon settles into itself to greet the gloaming. *Le bouchon* literally means wine cork, but it is also a kind of bistro which serves a less haughty fare than a *L'auberge*-style bistro, and this particular stew is one that will fill and warm a man who has been lost in the woods in winter and after two days has found his way to the porch of a country inn where the cook, a rotund woman in a cotton frock over which lies a white apron splattered with stains of tomatoes, opens the door with a wooden spoon in her hand, and her smile reveals the warmth of the fire over which a large pot of stew simmers and wafts within.

I add a quartered onion in which I have embedded four whole cloves, and then celery and carrots and bay leaves, and I bring this to a boil and then let it relax to a simmer where it will linger for the next three hours. This country dish has been one of considerable contention during the last few centuries: there are those in the Languedoc region who decidedly declare lamb to be a constitutional component of the stew while others say that the inherently integral ingredient is goose. Those in Bordeaux are in favor of duck and pork, and me, I favor pork shoulder, plump pork sausages, smoked ham hocks and a whole domesticated duck.

While the beans continue to stew atop the gas range, I mince garlic, my favorite food. If I were a poet, I would write an ode to garlic for it is as deserving of one as any Grecian urn. Maybe I'll suggest this to Gunnar for he, too, is an afficionado of *Allium sativum*, that most hardy plant of the amaryllis family. *Your languid stem does not reveal/secret bulbs beneath the ground/cloves in white papered mounds/explode alone a treasured meal....* The poignant aroma of garlic sends me traveling through meals I have had and have yet to have, and now, as the knife does its quick dance, my hunger becomes whole.

I dice four tomatoes and I chop parsley, and I think the language of cooking is the most beautiful there is, the chopping and dicing and mincing, the julienne, the simmer and sauté; it is a poetic ballet. I do not enjoy cooking for myself nearly as much as I do cooking for others with whom I will dine, and this pleasure I have in cooking this *cassoulet* for my wife and good friends is divine. There are so many therapies for those who are clinically depressed, but I wonder if anyone has studied the efficacy of cooking. Surely to prepare a fine meal for good friends and family is the cure for the deepest doldrums.

I pour a little olive oil in the bottom of the Dutch oven and I sauté the garlic for a couple of minutes before adding the tomatoes and parsley and a dab of tomato paste which I sauté for a few more minutes before I add the pork shoulder and the ham hocks and over this I pour three cups of an oaky Chardonnay. After bringing this to a boil, I put on the lid and set this in the oven at 375 degrees, and I am done until an hour and a half before dinner when I will add the sausage and the duck, and when this is done I will pour this over a bed of beans on which I will then sprinkle bread crumbs. All this will go into a 450 degree oven for twelve minutes and, voila, dinner will be served. Oh, the juices in my stomach prepare themselves already for I am now as hungry as I have ever been.

Bacchus is lying under the kitchen table, asleep and snoring. I enjoy watching a sleeping dog lie, and I wonder how her brain works.

Does she dream of our last hunt and is she haunted in nightmare by that magical goose that disappeared before her eyes, her jaw? She will wake soon, will Bacchus, for it is not often that she naps and when she does it is for a short time only. She will smell the aroma of the meats cooking in their tomato sauce, and she, too, will grow hungry.

As I wash the dishes, I wonder why people think they are the masters of this universe. Isn't it that dogs have it much better than do we? We brush them and comb them and wash them and walk them and feed them and water them and shelter them, and when they are ill, we take them to the vet. What is it that we do for each other? Not nearly as much. And it is the dogs of this world who are truly in awe of that which surrounds them, much more than we. Lao Tsu said, *When men lack a sense of awe, there will be disaster*. And we have seen disaster in all its various guises and it seems that we are only in awe of them, the guises.

I hear the garage door opening. So does Bacchus for she opens her eyes, lifts her head, tilts it to one side, sits, stands, runs to the door that leads to the garage and she wags her tail in expectation. Etsuko is home. I turn off the tap, wipe the counters. Bacchus barks. "Easy, girl," I say. The door opens and there is my wife of twenty-five years.

"It smells wonderful. Hello, there, Bacchus." She bends and pets Bacchus who immediately lies down for a belly rub. "Look at your dog," she says to me, and I walk over and give her a kiss, the dog on the floor between us. "Good thing she's spaded. She's an easy shit."

I like it when Etsuko swears. She has learned these words from me and she employs them in her own particular idiomatic fashion. She doesn't often swear, but when she does, it makes me smile and it reminds me that I have taught her a few things as she has me. That first day so long ago when I was teaching her how to drive a manual transmission and she was having trouble getting it into gear, I was impatient and I shouted that she was going to ruin the clutch. She turned the ignition off and shouted back at me, "Suck my dick." She'd heard me say that to a driver who'd cut me off, but I hadn't bothered to explain that Dick was more than the diminutive of Richard.

43

She sets her purse on the counter. "What time are they coming?"

"Five."

"Then I'd better hurry. That's a little over an hour."

"Hurry where?"

"A shower."

I follow her down the hall to the bathroom where she disrobes before me. After all of these years, the sight of her body still roils my loins. She turns on the shower, climbs in, closes the door behind her and I am left standing alone.

"How are things at the university?" I say as I quietly remove my own pants, let them fall to the floor. Then my boxers.

"Nothing new."

The water rushes, steam rising above the door.

"And the students? They continue to work hard?" I pull off my socks.

"Yes and no," she says, her voice hollowed by Italian tile. "You know how they are."

"How's Madame The Chair?" I unbutton my shirt, withdraw from the sleeves and then pull off my undershirt, drop it onto the pile so that now I am naked yet hardly stark.

"Still concerned about enrollment. She lives and breathes FTE. She...Jake, now Jake, we don't have much time," and I close the door behind me and embrace my soapy sweet.

The guests have arrived. We've had our cocktails in the living room before the fire—Karla, she had the gin fizz; Etsuko the margarita on the rocks, no salt; both Gunnar and I a neat Scotch with a glass of porter back–and we are now at the dining room table, and having finished the spinach salad, I have served the main course.

Karla is a tall drink of water, as they say, with long black hair streaked with gray, sparkling brown eyes, and high cheekbones. She has a sincere curiosity about everything and is the sort of person who, upon meeting you for the first time, will ask you how you feel about death.

She is not morbid, exactly; she just wants to know things other people ignore. Once she asked me about my first orgasm and I remember blushing through my stuttered response.

She and Gunnar are an odd pair, I've always thought. Karla is the webmaster for a high tech firm and Gunnar is a romantic poet. Ah, love is mysterious. They have been married some fifteen years, Gunnar's first and Karla's second. Her first husband was physically abusive and once they separated she secured a restraining order which he regularly broke and on Halloween he showed up on her doorstep dressed in a devil costume. When she opened the door, he forced his way in and he beat her all the way into the kitchen where she grabbed a butcher knife and stabbed him in the back. Seven times. This I learned from Gunnar.

Gunnar is fifty-five and Karla is forty-five. They met in Gunnar's undergraduate poetry class. Her therapist suggested she take a poetry class, and I can remember Gunnar–the confirmed bachelor back then–coming to my office to tell me of this student, "Karla Sweethorn, the most beautiful woman I have ever seen."

"Gunnar, you say that every quarter. You're always falling in love."

"No, it's true. If it's possible to be smitten, then I am smitten to the core. I may swoon from this day on."

"How's her poetry?"

"Terrible. She'll never be a poet. She has no poetic sensibility. But, my God, she's got a poetic body. Beautiful."

A year later they were married and she, like Gunnar, became our very best friend. They have no children due, in large part, to the reversible vasectomy Gunnar had twenty years ago when he first foresaw the overpopulation we suffer from now, but if he has changed his mind about crowd control it would be to no avail for the doctor slipped up and the vasectomy got stuck in first gear.

"The stew is wonderful, Jake," Karla says. She sits to my left, Gunnar to my right and Etsuko sits at the opposite end of the table. Bacchus lies before the fire in the living room. Although she is given free reign of the house, we do not allow her at table when we dine.

We had one of our own Pinot gris' with the salad and I've poured us all a glass of a '97 Pinot noir to accompany the stew. I take a bite of the duck and find it succulent. "Jake," Etsuko says. "It's delicious."

"Thank you. Gunnar, would you pass the bread?"

Gunnar wipes his mouth with a napkin, passes the bread. "Have you written the review?"

I frown. "Gunnar, I've panned the book. I'm sorry. It's terrible."

For a moment, he looks stunned. Then he resumes eating, looking at his plate. "That quite all right. You're professional." I catch eyes with Etsuko and then Karla. Gunnar, he is so damned gullible.

"There was nothing in the book to like," I say. "I'm surprised Norton published it. I guess it was on the strength of your last book. The sonnets have no life. The one villanelle rang false, and that sestina, well why bother?"

Gunnar takes a sip of wine. "Could be," he says.

"Gunnar," I say.

Still Karla and Etsuko are silent, both of them watching the two of us.

He concentrates on his food, won't look at me. "Yes?"

I reach over and slap him on the back. "Damn, Gunnar, you're gullible. That's your best work yet, you know, and I wrote a review positively effusive. Shit, I ought to get a commission."

He looks at me and smiles. "You are a good friend."

I lift my wine glass. "To friends," I say. And we toast. I pour more wine.

"How's your writing going?" Karla asks me.

I finish chewing a piece of bread. It is a crusty baguette and I am generous with the butter. "It's going well."

"How many pages today?" Karla asks.

"Five."

"How much do you usually do in a day?" Still Karla.

"Five pages, rain or shine. Twenty-five a week."

"How far along are you now?"

"Well, Gunnar, I'm about forty-seven pages in."

"I know you don't like to talk about your work in progress, but just a hint of what it's about? The plot? The conflict?"

"Karla, Karla, Karla. Wait until the movie comes out. No, really. It's about friends and family. Love between a husband and wife. Man's best friend, the loyal dog. It's about a man trying to discern where he is and how he got there. Even why. Nothing ground breaking. No submarines or nuclear battles or mysterious deaths. Today I wrote about cooking *cassoulet le bouchon*. Say that. *Cassoulet le bouchon.* Say that. In French. With the accent. Try it. It's like traveling. *Cassoulet le bouchon.* Oh, that's fun. Go ahead, Karla."

"*Cassoulet le bouchon.*" She smiles. "*Cassoulet le bouchon.*" She laughs, sips her wine. "That is something. And I don't speak French."

"Etsuko, try it," I say. "*Cassoulet le bouchon.* Go ahead now. You'll like it."

"Well..."

"Go on," Karla says. "*Cassoulet le bouchon,*" she says with a very exaggerated accent as she pinches her nose between thumb and forefinger for accentuation, and then she starts to giggle.

"*Cassoulet le bouchon,*" Etsuko says and laughs self-consciously. "Not a very good accent, I guess."

"No, it's fine," I say. "Really, try it again. *Cassoulet le bouchon.*"

"*Cassoulet le bouchon,*" she says again, this time with more Je ne sais quois because of the tweaked nose. "*Cassoulet le bouchon.*" She giggles, too.

"Gunnar, you try it," Karla says. "*Cassoulet le bouchon.*"

"I don't know."

"Gunnar," I say. "Take a sip of wine and say it. It'll be like traveling in France for the moment the words curl off your tongue." I get up and retrieve another bottle of wine from the counter. "Go on."

"Okay, I guess. *Cassoulet le bouchon.*"

Karla laughs. Etsuko smiles. I laugh.

"See, you're mocking me."

"No, no, no," I say.

"We're not," Karla says.

"You said it so well," Etsuko says.

"One more time, Gunnar, or I won't mail out the review."

"That's blackmail."

"Touche."

"*Cassoulet le bouchon.* There, I said it. Now are you happy?"

We are all laughing too hard to reply. Etsuko finds control first. "Gunnar, for a man of Swedish extraction, you do well with the French accent."

He pours himself more wine. I ladle more stew from the serving bowl in the center of the table. A piece of duck breast. Ham hock. More beans.

"How did we get onto this?" Gunnar says.

"You asked me what I wrote this morning. And I wrote," I hold my nose between my thumb and forefinger to improve my French accent, "*Cassoulet le bouchon.*"

We all laugh. "And what will you write tomorrow?" Karla asks.

"Something of a man's days in a far away country when he was young. But someday I will write of a dinner party where four friends amuse themselves by holding their noses and saying the name of a French stew in French. *Cassoulet le bouchon.*"

We all fall into fits of laughter and Etsuko tells Karla to be careful what she says for, she warns, it could well end up in what I write some day. Karla does not know the half of it; Etsuko, however, knows the whole.

I get up to put a log on the fire. Bacchus is stretched out on the rug before the fading embers. I lay down a piece of oak and the embers stir. Bacchus watches me with her brown eyes and I bend down and rub her soft fur beneath her chin, and then I return, sip more wine. Etsuko is telling Karla about *The Incident* of three weeks before when we were walking through the Park Blocks next to the university and we were

48

confronted by three skinheads. It is a sad tale, one that makes me both angry and sad. The boys were arrested.

"Is that the first time something like that's happened?" Gunnar asks.

"That overt," Etsuko says.

"Did you feel physically threatened, Jake, just upon seeing them?"

I think about it a moment. I did feel threatened. We had been in the library and were crossing the Park Blocks on our way to the Heathman for a drink. I saw the three young men, boys, whatever, walking towards us. They had shaved heads and they wore jeans and leather coats and they wore Doc Martens. As we passed, one of them said, "Hey, gook lover." I grabbed him by the throat and shoved him against a tree and the other two started beating me, kicking me, and Etsuko kicked at them.

"I don't know. I just reacted. Good thing the police were there." There were two patrolmen on horseback and they came and beat the boys off with night sticks. "The trial is next week."

"I hope they lock them up for the rest of their lives," Karla says.

"That's how I feel. But Etsuko, ask her what she wants to do."

Gunnar looks at Etsuko over the rim of his wine glass. "Well?" he says.

"She wants to have them over for dinner," I say.

"What's this?" Karla says. "Really, Etsuko? Dinner? With three racist thugs?"

"See?" I say to her.

"Locking them up won't do any good," she says. "So I want the judge to order them to come here for a traditional Japanese dinner."

"With tainted *fugu*," I say.

"That would be an interesting sentence," Karla says. "Me, I'd rather kill them."

"Karla," Gunnar says.

"Well, I would. Like that asshole in Grig's Hole last summer.

49

Kill him, too." Gunnar and Karla were traveling through eastern Oregon the summer before and had stopped for lunch in Grig's Hole. The owner of the cafe wouldn't serve them. He said he didn't serve "Squaws."

"We've made some progress in the last thirty years, but not as much as we think we've made," Gunnar says.

I hold my nose and say, "*Cassoulet le bouchon*," to change the tenor of our talk, but our smiles are without much cheer.

Karla, however, does not go for my attempt at the change of subjects. "Were you ever the victim of racism in Japan?" She asks me.

I take a sip of wine and look across the table at Etsuko. There were a few minor incidents, but never anything major. That's what I tell her.

"Give me a for instance then," she says.

"Well, once we were in a movie theater and there was a yakuza sitting behind us."

"A yakuza?" Gunnar says, reaching for more wine.

"Japanese mafia."

"How can you tell?" Karla asks.

"Tatoos. A short permanent of curly hair. A general surliness. Arrogance like roosters. That's the stereotype."

"And what happened?" Gunnar.

"Nothing much."

It had been a matinee in Shinjuku and the theater was mostly empty. This short muscular guy with curly hair sat down directly behind me when he could have sat anywhere. His arms were festooned with dragons and he had short curly hair. He was drunk and he smoked although smoking in theaters was forbidden. He kept kicking the back of my seat Whenever I turned to look at him, he would say sorry, and then he would kick the chair again. "And he would mumble things about foreigners taking away good Japanese women. He wasn't so much a *yakuza as a chimpera*."

"What's that?" Gunnar asks.

"A kind of wannabe *yakuza*. A loser."

"It is a very derogatory comment," Etsuko says with a severity unmatched this evening.

"So nothing else happened?" Karla asks.

"No. We just ignored him," I say. "There is racism in Japan, of course. But mostly it is covert. It is institutional. Seldom is it overt like the punks in the Park Blocks. The gentlemen whom Etsuko wants to have over for dinner."

She sends a glare my way, and I deserve it, but I do not think as does she that we can educate them over dinner.

We all have more stew and we talk about the winter we have weathered these past two months, the onslaught of rain day after day which is typical of an Oregon winter when the sky ceases to exist from November until April, and then one day the clouds are unzipped and there is a slice of blue sky to remind us that spring is gathering its forces and will arrive one day when it is least expected.

Karla has brought a cheesecake for desert and we drink espressos and Gunnar and I each have two Calvados', but we go easier than the last dinner when we got carried away and downed an entire bottle so that the next day neither of us was much good to write. "What's your next project?" I ask Gunnar.

"I thought I'd try a novel in haiku."

"Why would you do that?" I ask.

"That's what I said," Karla says.

"It sounds intriguing to me." Etsuko the diplomat.

"Well, Vikram Seth has already done it with sonnets."

"So what?" I say. "Why bastardize the novel by attempting to transmute its form? Who could read the million haiku it would take to complete the novel? It makes no sense."

"No? Maybe you're right." Gunnar sighs, takes a bite of cake. "I just thought it would be an interesting intellectual undertaking."

"Masturbation more like it," I say. "Delicious cake, Karla. Gunnar, why not write a novel as a novel? Or a collection of haiku. 'Under the cherry trees/Soup, the salad, fish and all..../Seasoned with petals.'"

"I've always liked that. Basho was elegant simplicity," Gunnar says.

"Who?" Karla asks.

I pour a tad more Calvados in first Gunnar's and then my glass with hurried stealth.

"Basho, Matsuo. Or Matsuo Basho here," Etsuko says. "In Japan, we say the family name first. A 17th century poet. He was writing of *hanami*. In April, we have cherry blossom viewing parties. You would call them picnics. We gather beneath the cherry trees when they are in bloom and we eat and drink throughout the day."

"Sounds like fun," Karla says.

"Believe me, it is," I say. "We used to gather with a group of about thirty friends and drink sake and beer and eat from noon until midnight. It was wonderful."

"Gunnar, you would have liked the earlier style," Etsuko says. "We have had *hanami* for more than fifteen centuries. In the sixteenth century, Toyotomi Hideyoshi took his military officers and poets to Yoshino where they wrote poems all day while watching the cherry blossoms."

"It sounds civilized," Gunnar says. He winks at me and drinks the Calvados.

"As was the dinner," Karla says. "But it is almost midnight and we need to let these good people go to bed." She stands and Gunnar stands, and that is the end of our night. It is always a pleasure to share a meal with Karla and Gunnar, and tonight was no exception.

We walk them out to their car accompanied by Bacchus. We hug and Karla climbs into the driver's seat, a sensible move considering how much Gunnar has drunk. They live in northwest Portland so they have a thirty minute drive before them.

Gunnar gives me a hug and thanks me again for the review.

"Shit, thank you for the poems. They are wonderful."

"Thanks for saying so. You really mean it?"

Etsuko takes me by the arm as Gunnar gets in the car. "Well, that one sestina was fairly lame, and the villanelle? Not worth mentioning."

He looks up at me and from his seat, pinches his nose and says, "*Cassoulet le bouchon.*" We both break into laughter at the same time, Estusko pulling me away as he pulls his door shut.

We stand in the cold and watch the red tail lights disappear down the drive until the two glowing orbs are but a reminder of their arrival, and I lean and kiss Etsuko on the lips. Bacchus, she barks and wags her tail. Good friends are the sum of our best hopes.

And then I whisper in Etsuko's ear, I whisper, "*Cassoulet le bouchon,*" and we walk arm in arm back to the house followed by the wagging dog.

•

It is amusing to look back on my life in searching for the turns I have made that have led me to be where I now stand. Amusing. I reiterate that writing a memoir can be the most vainglorious of activities unless it is done for the proper reason which is to put your house in order so that you can find those things you need. I am reconstructing my life merely so that I can understand who and why I am who I am today. It is something everyone should do because it will serve as a reminder of how you should live out the remainder of your days.

I went to Japan because I was bored. I had returned from my service in Africa as a Peace Corps volunteer and I spent time as a newspaper reporter on a small weekly on the Oregon coast, and I still had the urge to travel, to visit nooks and crannies of the world (as I still wish to do today), so when I saw the ad asking for English teachers in Japan, I jumped on it, and the rest, as they say, is history. I am married to Etsuko and have begotten a beautiful daughter because one Sunday morning so many years ago, I happened across an ad in *The Sunday Oregonian* describing the need of someone to teach at a conversation school in Ichikawa on the outskirts of Tokyo.

We in the west are obsessed with causal relationships, but there is not always a discernibly direct cause to any given effect. Our universe is random and chaotic at best and to believe that everything we do is an explicable cause to some discernable effect is sheer naive arrogance. Lao Tsu wrote, *That which shrinks/Must first expand./That which fails/Must first be strong./That which is cast down/Must first be raised./Before receiving/There must be giving./This is called the perception of the nature of things./Soft and weak overcome hard and strong./Fish cannot leave deep waters,/And a country's weapons should not be displayed.*

Far too many memoirs are polished cannons on the border of the writer's ego.

I will say only this: I am damn glad that I was bored all those years ago. Thus, at best the cause of my present existence was the sufficient provocation of ennui.

After we married, we returned to our Ichikawa apartment for we were still in the throes of the school year and I had to teach. Etsuko worked in Tokyo at Sony so some mornings we rode the crowded trains together. At rush hour the platform was packed with men and women waiting to step through the pneumatic doors, and those at the end of the line would be shoved in by conductors who with their white gloved hands would push in any appendages that stuck out of the sliding doors.

It was at my first *hanami* that I met Etsuko who had come back from graduate school in China and was in Ichikawa visiting a friend. I had been invited to *hanami* by Toshichan, the master of Bonard's, a little jazz bar on Daimon Dori that I had gone into for a beer my first week in Japan when the only word of Japanese I knew was sayonara. It was at Bonard's that I studied Japanese, but imagine how difficult it was to get to know anyone when the only word I knew was *goodbye*.

Before I discovered Bonard's, I thought the Japanese word *hai* meant hello so that when I went to the green grocer for vegetables and he said "*Hai*," I quite naturally said "Hi," to which he responded, "*Hai?*" and I "Hi" once more. As I did not know the word meant yes and was a standard greeting to customers, I thought the poor man hard of hearing and I raised my voice several decibels before realizing that the word must not mean hello.

It is strange that if you know only two languages, as did I at the time, that you immediately revert to your second language when addressed in a language you do not understand; thus, when I walked in restaurants and bars and shops during those first few days before my instruction began at Bonard's, I would automatically respond in French to any query and thus it was I carried on long conversations with the vendors on Daimon Dori, conversations in which neither party could understand the other, yet conversations they were as we gestured until the requisite fruits and vegetables were finally found.

"*Konnichiwa.*"

"*Bonjour, Madame.*"

"*Hai?*"

"*Oui.*"

"*Nanini shimasuka?*"

"*Est ce que vous avez des pommes du terre?*"

"*Wakarimasen.*"

"*Je ne comprehend pas, Madame.*"

"*Wakarimasen.*"

"*Sayonara.*"

"*Sayonara.*"

The latter being the only word that was mutually understood.

It had been my fourth day of teaching and I was tired. I finished the day with a nine o'clock class comprised of three businessmen, Hiroshi, Hideki and Satoru. I was giving them a lesson on the present perfect and had written *Subject + Have + Past Participle + Object* on the white board. I was teaching in the middle and largest classroom that consisted of a sofa and four chairs. Immediately outside the sliding door sat Kyoko, the secretary who I believed spent the preponderance of her day eavesdropping and then reporting any digressions on the part of the three American teachers to her husband, the school's director.

"Okay, a little grammar," I said.

Hiroshi raised his hand. This was my third night teaching this class, and Hiroshi annoyed me with his allegiance to propriety. "Hiroshi," I said. "You don't need to raise your hand. This is a conversation school and we don't raise our hands in the middle of conversations."

"Sorry." He pulled down his hand and looked sheepish at my mild reprimand.

"Did you get your promotion?" I asked him. He was supposed to find out that afternoon.

"No. No promotion."

"I'm sorry. I thought it was a done deal."

"Done deal?" Hideki said as he wrote the phrase in his notebook.

"In the bag," I said.

"In the bag?" Hideki asked as he wrote that down as well. Meanwhile Satoru stayed quiet. He hardly ever spoke. He was shy and his pronunciation was garbled.

"Already assured. Now what was your question?"

"Question?" Hiroshi asked.

"Yes. You had your hand up."

"Ah. Is present perfect?"

"I'd hardly say that. And neither was the past."

"What?" Hiroshi said, disappointed. "Not present perfect."

"Is joke, Hiroshi-san. Jake-sensei make joke," Hideki said.

"Joke?" Satoru said. It sounded like jockey.

"Joke," Hideki said. "Funny boy. This new teacher, Jake-san, he is funny boy." And Hideki started to laugh. "Ha, ha. You certainly funny boy."

"Yes, Hiroshi," I said. "I was making a joke. Making light of a very serious question. Please forgive me."

"Is okay," Hiroshi said. "American joke is good joke."

"Let's begin, then. Hiroshi, have you eaten dinner?"

"Not reasonable question, I think, Jake-sensei. See," he looked at his watch, "it is only ten o'clock. I not eat dinner until eleven."

"Hiroshi," I said. "This is only an example. We are practicing the present perfect. It's a tense."

"Ah," Hideki said. "Relax."

"Relax?"

"Like Satoru-san." Hideki elbowed Satoru who I saw had fallen asleep. "You said tense. I make joke."

I sighed. "Beautiful. You make joke. Can we practice, everybody? Can we? We only have a few minutes left."

"May we," Hiroshi said.

"May we what?" I said.

"You say can we, I say may we. Sorry, your habit," Hiroshi said.

"Okay. *May* we practice. Hiroshi, have you eaten dinner?"

"I told you no. Too early."

"Fine, but you are supposed to say, 'No, I haven't.' It's the present perfect."

Hideki smiled and said, "We practice the present perfect, we make future nicer."

"Very good, Hideki. Have you eaten dinner?"

"No, I haven't." He turned to Satoru, elbowing him in the ribs. "Have you been to sex shows in Shinjuku?"

Satoru's eyes brightened. "Yes, I have." He turned to Hiroshi. "Hiroshi, have you been to sex shows?"

Hiroshi frowned. "No, I haven't," he said and turned to me. "Have you been to Tokyo Disneyland?" He asked me.

"No, I haven't. But I have been to Disneyland in California."

"Is it good?" Hideki asked.

"It's okay," I said.

"Do you like Japanese girl?" Hideki continued.

"Girls."

"Ah," Hideki said. "More than one? You have many?"

"No. You said *girl*. You are supposed to say girls."

"Okay," Hideki said. Satoru and Hiroshi were paying more attention now. "Do you like Japanese *girls*?"

"Yes, I do."

"Me, I like American girl," Satoru said.

"Me, too," Hideki said.

"I have no girl friend," Hiroshi said.

"That's too bad," I said. "I'm sure you will have a girl friend someday."

"No, girls no like me."

"Why?"

"I don't know."

"Let's practice present perfect, Jake-sensei," Hideki said. "Jake-sensei, have you had sex many times?"

I didn't now how to respond to his question, but I could see all three men eagerly awaited my response so I replied in the affirmative. The truth was, I had probably had sex with fewer women than most young men.

"How many?" Hideki asked.

"I don't know."

"I like girls with small, how do you say this?" Hideki asked as he grabbed his ankle.

"Ankle."

"Yes, with small ankles."

"I think we should call it a night," I said. "Things are deteriorating."

"Of course," Hiroshi said. "It is night. We call it a night because it is night."

I could see he was serious. "No, I said. 'Call it a night' means the day is over."

"Of course," Hiroshi said. "Night is when day is finished."

I looked at my watch. It was 10:30. Our lesson was finished. "It means we are done."

"We are done," Hiroshi said and stood, and the others followed his lead.

"All right," Hideki said. "Thank you, Jake-sensei. We're tits up."

I must have looked surprised for he said he had a book of

American idioms that he was studying and that one he had liked the best.

I walked up Daimon Dori toward my apartment and upon arriving before Bonard's, I heard a mournful saxophone and what sounded like convivial conversation emanating from the door. After a long day of teaching, I was ready for a beer. I opened the door and went in.

●

I have been writing an hour and feel somewhat invigorated by the memories of Japan as I sit here in my office in Banks, Bacchus at my feet snoring with a certain dyspeptic disposition. After Gunnar and Karla left last night, I gave Bacchus a small bowl of the stew over which I poured not more than four ounces of Pinot noir to help settle her stomach though I fear I caused a minor uproar. The Great Northern beans have had a flatulent effect and between snores she farts so that the gas serves as percussion to her bass.

Etsuko is grading papers in her study on this Saturday morning. She is waiting for me to finish writing and once I have, we will go to Portland today to buy a new futon for Etsuko does not want to risk having her parents sleep on the bed in the guest room for fear of falling as she once did when we stayed at my parents' on her first visit from Japan. The next morning, my parents asked what the crash in the middle of the night had been, and I laughed and told them that Etsuko had fallen out of bed. She, being embarrassed, told them I pushed her, something I think they believed.

Sometimes when in the middle of a writing session, I will stop, cradle my chin in the palm of my left hand, my left elbow bowed on the arm rest of my chair, and I will let my mind wander. It is not unlike unleashing Bacchus. My mind roars off as does the dog, sniffing memories in many directions, and when it happens upon a good one, I retrieve it and jot it down in my notebook for later use.

I do this now and I think of many things: a drunk swim across the Edogawa in Tokyo; a motorcycle ride into Tokyo and a police escort out of the Imperial Palace, the grounds of which I had inadvertently entered; a motorcycle trip to the northernmost island of Hokkaido where I lasted a week on twenty dollars by sleeping in train stations. All of these episodes must be included in the memoir, or at least a large portion of them. I told Cindy I would have the manuscript finished by the end of the month, and I believe I shall. I almost never miss a deadline. My punctuality is in many ways a Calvinistic handicap, I believe, for I miss out on much in life by being gripped by clock and calendar. When I was very young, my father taught me how to back up the time so as never to be late, and while he had the best intentions for a young boy, I am not altogether sure he should not have mitigated his admonition about tardiness with a word about smelling the roses when in bloom for in many ways punctuality is the real thief of time. Just think of how we would like to procrastinate the big hook of death! (I hope this is the only exclamation mark I have used in this manuscript. I have seen student work where they are sprinkled in like salt and pepper and for years I admonished the students, but only knew why subconsciously until I heard what Mark Twain said on the matter: Using an exclamation mark is like laughing at your own joke.)

Etsuko and I spent a day at the beach two weeks ago. It was a rare day in December when the sun was out and there was an absence of winter storm. We sat on a nest of driftwood watching the waves crash onto the beach, watching them die and then retreat with a timidity so great in comparison with their arrival. It was as if they arrived like a brash young man at a party only to be told by the hostess he had not been invited. We watched as a young boy bent at water's edge, writing his name into the sand with a stick of driftwood. When he was done, the water crept back between his legs and effaced what he had written. He turned and watched the wave that had stolen his name, and it was as if he were watching himself sixty or seventy years in the future, watching himself be swept away by the tide that is life and death. Then he turned back to the sand in what I thought an act of defiance, and he once again wrote his name into the sand. And I thought: That is life: A continual act of what is ultimately futile defiance, and though I continue to defy, I realize that the tide is closing in.

That night when we returned home, I wrote a short poem about the boy writing his name in the wet sand. It is not a particularly good poem, I fear, but it is one from the heart without florid guise. Gunnar and I had a discussion of this not long ago, a discussion of those whom I refer to as academic poets who write verse that cannot be readily understood for it is replete with pedantic esoterica so arcane that the average reader would need a translator to get through the poem. And what is the sense in that? Gunnar agreed and said he felt that some of these poets are without an iota of self confidence so that they feel it necessary to delude their readers into thinking that he, the poet, is so much smarter than is he, the reader, when it is obviously the other way around.

•

When I opened the door, I was greeted by a waft of cigarette smoke and all seven bar patrons turned to see who had come in. When they saw me, they looked surprised and then they turned back to their drinks. The room was smaller than the average bedroom and there was no room for tables. The walls were festooned with colorfully painted kites and two huge speakers hung from the ceiling. The bar itself was the shape of an L and there were eight bar stools, all but one occupied. I took a seat at the foot of the L next to the wall and the bartender steadfastly ignored my presence as he was engaged in conversation with another of the patrons.

"I'd like a beer," I said in English, and the man next to me, a rough looking fellow with a mop of unkempt hair, smiled and said, "*Beeru.*" I noticed he was missing one of his front teeth.

"Yes, *beeru,*" I said.

He then said something to the bartender who came and said something to me and I said, "*Beeru*."

"*Beeru hoshii desu ka?*"

I hadn't the faintest as to what he was saying so I said, "Yes."

"*Hai* is yes," this same man on my right said. "Say *hai*."

"*Hai*," I said although I still did not know what it was I was saying yes to.

"And *kudasai* is please."

"*Hai, beeru kudasai*," I said.

He brought me a bottle of Sapporo and a glass and I knew then that I had found the right bar. Toshichan was the bartender's name and this was the first of many nights of Japanese lessons played out before the backdrop of beer and the jazz he played on his stereo.

The man next to me said, "You American?"

"*Hai*, I am American."

"I Japanese."

"I thought as much," I said.

"What?"

"*Hai*, you Japanese."

He reached for my beer bottle and I thought he was going to drink it, but he tilted the bottle and refilled my glass. "Good beer," he said.

"*Hai*."

"What your name?"

"Jake Weedsong."

"Jake Weedsong-san?"

"Yes."

"Funny name."

"*Hai*."

Then he said something in Japanese to the rest of the patrons whom I could see were all acquaintances and I heard *Weedsong-san* mouthed by each of them and then everyone laughed.

"We like Weedsong-san. Is good name."

"Thank you."

"*Domo arrigato*," he said. "Is thank you."

"*Domo arrigato*."

"Good."

"What is your name?"

"Me?" And he looked surprised as he poured his own glass full of beer. "Me? I Matsuda."

"Matsuda-san?"

"Yes."

Soon I was the focus of attention as everyone tried their broken English on me asking me sundry questions about where I was from and what I was doing here, and as they talked Toshichan would occasionally interrupt and tell me the Japanese word for the English word I had used, and I realized then that the best way to learn a language was to not know you were learning it at all.

Matsuda-san pushed his plate of dried squid in front of me and said, "Eat," and Toschan said, "*Taberu*," and I ate and learned another word.

As it turned out, Toshichan was an archeologist by day and the owner of this small bar on top of which he and his wife had an apartment. Keiko was a book keeper whose passion was flamenco dancing, and she now sat at the end of the bar which she would do every night I was there as her husband stood on the other side cooking small dishes and pouring beer, sake and whiskey for the patrons who were all friends of different degree. As I sipped my beer and ate squid and *edamame*, I thought to myself, this is a poet's bar.

•

As I wrote that last passage, I went back in time and I was there in Bonard's drinking beer and smoking cigarettes, and I was young and carefree for the period it took to bang the words out on the keyboard. Now I sit and stare at those words on the screen and I am back in the present with Bacchus at my feet. I stretch. And I think: If you visit your past now and again, you mark your age, but if you stay wholly in the present there is no sense of time. In "Youth," Joseph Conrad wrote, "Only a moment; a moment of strength, of romance, of glamour–of youth!...A flick of sunshine upon a strange shore, the time to remember, the time for a sigh, and–goodbye!–Night–Goodbye...!"

And that is what this memoir is, occasions to live in the past. It may not be that anyone will want to read this, but that is all right. The very writing of it is a fulfillment of its own. I will say, however, that in writing this, that in any of my writing, doubt sneaks from the shadows from time to time, the doubt that this is any good and that maybe I should be writing something else, a thriller, for example, and I suppose all writers share this feeling, the feeling of *is this even worth the bother*? I suppose all artists share that feeling from time to time, or should I say all people for we all are pursued by that great evil angst and it does upon occasion catch us and bring us down.

How to avoid it other than to be fully engaged at every task at hand?

We are standing with a small crowd of people waiting for friends and family to appear from the behind the wall where the recently arrived passengers are going through customs. Etsuko's grip of my hand is tight. She is nervous. Her parents have never been out of Japan and here they are going through customs at Portland International Airport. As we wait, I am hoping that nothing untoward happens on the other side of that wall, but with the American INS, one can never be sure as they seem to believe that they are each and every one the dictators of a country to themselves.

"They must be exhausted," I say to Estsuko.

"They will be tired, yes," she says.

"We'll take them straight home and ply them with drinks and I'll barbecue the flank steak and after we eat, we'll send them straight to bed."

Etsuko stands tall on her toes and kisses me on the cheek. "I love you, Jake."

I first hug and then kiss her. "And I love you."

Then we see first her mother and then her father. He is as dapper as he ever was dressed in a dark suit with a blue tie neatly knotted over his white shirt. His hair, once jet black but now streaked with flecks of gray, is carefully parted and gelled in place. He walks with the careful posture of a general inspecting his troops, his head turning from side to side, maybe in search of his daughter. And she, her mother, walks with a slight shuffle in her gray dress, and her smile sparkles from her gold tooth.

Etsuko bows before first her father and then her mother and then I do the same, and then I hug Mother and kiss her on the cheek so that she blushes deep red. "I love you," I tell her in Japanese, and she laughs and waves out her hand at me to ward off such amorous advances, and then the four of us walk out to the car.

The flank steak had been marinated in a brine of garlic, *mirin*, soy sauce and apple juice, and I barbecued it just three minutes on each side. We had steamed white rice for that is the integral part of every Japanese meal, as requisite as gasoline to the functioning of the internal combustion engine, and we drank a bottle of Pinot noir from two years ago, and even her father had a glass as it was our very own wine. We finished eating an hour ago and now the four of us are in the hot tub on the patio and the steam rises into the cold January night so that I feel like the four of us are in a witch's caldron being slowly stewed beneath the glimmering stars. But, I wonder, what would the witch have with us, two generations of people in love? Why turn us into anything other than what we are? What intentions?

I sit next to *Oto-san*, who yawns, and across from us sit Etsuko and her mother. I stretch my leg beneath the water's surface and watch Etsuko as my foot inches its way up her leg, and with my continued progress grows my horror for Etsuko's face reveals nothing in the way of acknowledgment. When I turn my shadowed gaze to *Okaa-san*, however, I see her fright in widely drawn eyes and I quickly withdraw my foot and say, "*Gomenasai, chigau ashi,*" sorry, wrong leg, and she smiles with a flash of gold and Etsuko asks what I am talking about, and father yawns again, and I say, "Etsuko, I was feeling up your mother's leg when I thought it to be yours," and she gives me a scowl and then smiles and tells her mother that I am a funny man.

●

There is a saying in Japan that the nail that stands up gets hammered down, and it seems to me that is the antithesis of everything American. Yet Americans don't always remember that when they visit another country they are guests and should behave as such. Japan is a mountainous country roughly the size of California with approximately 120 million residents. In other words, almost half the population of the U.S. in just one state. If everyone were rocking the boat, well, it wouldn't float for long is the point to that aphorism about the nail.

My good friend Larry Johnson was to meet me at Ichikawa's sports center which was located on the hill above Daimon Dori where I lived and it was there where we played basketball every Sunday evening. Outside was a soccer field and a track. It was a warm spring evening, and Larry and I decided to go early to toss around a football before everyone showed up for basketball which we would play for two hours or so before heading to Larry's house for beer.

Larry was sitting on a bench next to the field awaiting my arrival. I parked my motorcycle and we walked down the stairs to the grass field. We were passing the ball back and forth, running short and long routes, when one of the officials of the sports center came out and told us that we couldn't play football on the field.

"Why not?" Larry asked in Japanese. His was much better than mine as he had already been in the country for three years when I arrived. He, too, was married to a Japanese woman, and he had two children ages three and five.

"Because it is a soccer field," the official replied with a face devoid of any mirth.

"Well, we're just running on the field throwing a ball, pretty much the same as soccer," Larry said. "Except with our hands, not our feet." He grinned.

"You cannot play football on a soccer field. You must stop at once. This is not a football field. It is a soccer field."

"You have to be kidding," Larry said.

"No."

"You don't see how ridiculous this is?"

"No. I only see two men playing football on a soccer field. Now, no more."

He turned and went back up the steps toward the gym, and we did the same, both of us bewildered at his not being able to see through our eyes how silly it seemed; but then, we didn't make much effort to see that soccer field he cared for through his eyes, either.

Twelve people showed up for basketball that night, nine Americans and three Japanese. We played five on five full court, shuffling in the two reserves. Although we never really practiced as such, we came together as a team three or four times a year whenever there was a tournament at the sports center. We even had jerseys with our name written boldly across the front in large kanji characters. We called ourselves *Yabanjin*, and to many of the officials who refereed our games, we were that: the hairy barbarians.

Later that night after a few beers at Larry's, I convinced him it would be a good idea to ride to Tokyo's Roppongi District on my motorcycle. Roppongi was the center for night life activities and it never shut down.

"Have you ever ridden your bike into Tokyo?" Larry wanted to know. Ichikwawa was in Chiba Prefecture, just across the Edo River from the great city.

"No. That's why I thought it would be fun."

I don't know why I thought I could find Roppongi, but Larry

agreed, so we went. Tokyo's streets had been deliberately constructed in a labyrinthine fashion so as to forestall any forces bent on invading the palace at the city's center, and here we were, somewhat inebriated, planning an invasion of our own.

Larry took a last sip of beer from his glass, stood and said, "Let's go."

•

I am up early today as we plan to take a trip to the coast. Everyone is still asleep save for Bacchus and me, and she lies at my feet looking at me with her pathetic up-rolled eyes which plead for me to finish typing, which I have. I think back through the spiral of years to that night when Larry and I rode to Roppongi and I smile. I have so many rich memories, yet I do not know how time has smudged them; in fact, I am incapable of this knowledge. This brings to mind sketchy lines from T.S. Eliot's masterpiece *The Four Quartets*, I think it was *Burnt Norton*: "Footfalls echo in the memory/Down the passage which we did not take/Towards the door we never opened/Into the rose garden." Why this comes to mind on this January morning, I can't be sure, and the irony, I suppose, is that I do not know if I have recalled those lines correctly. Ha! Etsuko is right: I am a *funny* man. There are times when I find myself amusing in the strangest of ways.

After having breakfast, I load the car. As soon as I open the tailgate, Bacchus jumps in the back. She loves to go for drives and hates to be left behind. I hadn't planned on her accompanying us today, and I think she senses this for as I stand next to the bumper, she lies down, head on the floor between both paws, her brown eyes frowned in despair. "Yes, Bacchus, you can go," I say, and immediately her tails goes all awag.

I drive with Father in the front next to me and our wives chatting in the back. It is an unusual day for January in the Coast Range: sunny and relatively warm. We drive through the thick forest and I can sense that Father is impressed with its density. I drive with a smile as I feel just plain good, content that I am in this car on this road with these people and my dog, that there is nowhere else in the world I could wish to be now. Lao Tsu wrote: *"Better stop short than fill to the brim./Oversharpen the blade, and the edge will soon blunt./Amass a store of gold and jade, and no one can protect it./Claim wealth and titles, and disaster will follow./Retire when the work is done./This is the way of heaven."*

As I recall those lines, my body is on auto-pilot and I cannot tell you of the curves we have driven through for my mind is drifting elsewhere. Then I come out of this trance, and I hear Etsuko telling her mother about the impending sentencing of the three skinheads and all my peace is gone.

"How terrible," I hear her mother say in Japanese.

"They should be sent to prison," her father says.

"Do you know what your daughter plans on recommending to the judge?" I say.

"Etsuko, tell them."

We have reached the summit of the Coast Range now and are descending the western slope. In a meadow surrounded by great Douglas Firs with skinny alders jabbing skyward through their branches, I see a herd of about twenty elk and I slow to a stop. There are three bulls standing tall among the grazing cows and calves. We watch them in silence for several minutes before I pull back onto the road. "Etsuko," I say and we make eye contact in the rearview mirror. "Tell them."

She does.

"You want to have them to dinner?" Her mother says.

"What good would that do?" Her father wants to know. "They could be dangerous."

"What good would prison do?" My lovely and stubborn wife asks. "They would come out the same as they went in. Worse."

"And you think dinner, a traditional Japanese dinner, will cure them of their hate?" Father asks. "I had not known of such medicinal qualities of sukiyaki."

"I don't know," she admits. "But it is better than shutting the problem away by sending them into prison for several years and then have them come out the same as before, probably worse."

No one says anymore on the subject, and I am relieved. As a rule, I avoid conflict as much as I can. I suppose that is why I prefer the company of Bacchus to all save my few close friends. Bacchus is at extreme peace with herself and when I go for a walk with her, I, too, can leave problems behind as I watch the wag of her tail, the swing of her hips, as she noses the air for the hidden secrets of time. I recall an aphorism by the twentieth century Spanish writer, Ramon Gomez De La Serna: "Dogs are always sniffing for the master they had in another life," and immediately I am jealous.

We cut south on Highway One, pass Cannon Beach, and then wrap around the shoulder of Neahkanie Mountain with the surf crashing several hundred yards beneath us. In the short distance we can see Nehalem Bay where we are going to go crabbing, something I have done since I was a child when my father and my uncle would takes us across the bay to the sandy spit where we would make a fire and set up a camp of sorts as they went out on the water to retrieve the crab pots they had dropped off. We would play on the beach and then cook what my uncle referred to as "mosties"–crabs that were almost of legal size–and in a cauldron of boiling water that hung above the fire we had made, boil them until their shells turned cherry red.

We have rented a boat from the Jetty Fishery which is situated close to the jaws of the bay itself. The water is calm on this incoming tide and after an hour we have seven keepers. Etsuko's mother is full of laughter as I maneuver the boat to an orange buoy, spray coming over the bow and dampening her hair. Father leans over and takes the buoy in his hands and I tell him to brace himself as I gun the engine into the tide as he reels in the slack rope the tide has carried along the water's surface until we are directly above the crab pot and he pulls hard, hand over hand, that slippery rope blistering his fine fingers.

He lifts the pot into the boat and sets it down. The crabs scurry out and along the floorboards. Father and I grab the crabs from behind and we drop the smaller ones and the females over the side. The keepers we put in the well under the seat and we can hear their claws scratch against the aluminum as they try to escape, fingernails on blackboard.

Once back at the car, Bacchus is beside herself with glee. She goes through contortions of happiness that almost disrobe her of her own skin. We sit on a log in the low winter sun as the proprietor cooks our crab in a huge vat of boiling water. Across the bay we watch a pod of seals sun themselves on the beach near the river's mouth. As I sip my beer, again memory encroaches on the present and I think of how I caught my first salmon in this river when I was twelve, how I told my father I thought I had a snag, how the salmon shot out of the water, my father saying, "That's some snag." Then I wonder what my three companions are thinking until father asks, "Do you hunt those seals?"

"No," I say. "They are protected."

"Protected from what?"

"People."

"Why is that?" He turns to look at me.

"I don't honestly know."

He sighs what seems to be a sense of dissatisfaction at my answer and we are called over to clean our crabs.

I break off the back shell, and take a sip of the yellow juices that lie in its curvature. This is what we call crab butter, I tell them, and then they try it too. It is resplendent of the sea, but so rich and thick that I make a conscious effort to widen my arteries. Then I show them how to pick out the crab's star-shaped heart and dip it in the juices, and we all try one before cleaning the rest of the crab.

We drive south through Garibaldi and then stop in Bay City to buy four dozen live oysters, and then on up the Wilson River Highway where Gunnar's friend, now deceased, the great poet William Stafford, set his poem "Traveling Through the Dark." Every time I drive this serpentine road, usually to fish the Wilson River for steelhead in January or February when it can be so cold that the water on the rod's eyelets freezes solid, I think of the poem and I remember the persona's struggle about what he should do that night when he finds a dead deer on the side of the road, one that is pregnant with a still-alive fawn. The last couplet reads: "I thought hard for us all–my only swerving–,/then pushed her over the edge into the river."

Sometimes responsibility runs right after you, I think, begging to be taken on. And this thought leads me through the labyrinth that is my mind to this: Maybe, just maybe, Etsuko is right. We'll show those skinheads our common humanity. Dinner it shall be!

•

Larry hung on as we drove through the nearly deserted streets. When we stopped at a light, he leaned forward and asked, "Are we there yet?" To which I laughed and said, "No. And neither is Gertrude Stein."

"What's that supposed to mean?"

"She's the one who said about Oakland, there's no there there."

"So?"

"Exactly." And I put it in gear, let out the clutch and roared off into the darkness.

We rode in the direction of my whims. I went straight until I found what I considered to be a promising street and then I turned left and continued on until a right turn seemed somehow appropriate and we proceeded in the fashion people use when trying to find the center of a maze, zig-zagging through the night in search of some bright neon light.

We had been driving for about thirty minutes when I turned right on a two-lane avenue that went through a large gate. I heard a shout and three uniformed men stepped in front of me. I hit the brakes. We were immediately surrounded by a dozen policemen. I had unwittingly entered the Imperial Palace and these men were bound to stop me from waking the Emperor.

I sat astride the bike as did Larry. "I think I fucked up, Larry."

"I think so, too," he said. And then added gratuitously, "Big time."

"Play your best dumb American."

"What could be dumber than this?"

One of the officers asked me, in Japanese, where I was going.

"I'm sorry," I said. "I don't speak Japanese."

The man said something I did not understand to his colleagues all of whom were standing in a circle around us. We were penned in. Then he turned to me. "Where you go?" He asked in English.

"Roppongi," I said. "We go to Roppongi." I don't know why it is that we cripple our own syntax when we speak to those who have a less than firm grip on our own language, but nevertheless, that is how I spoke. Is it that we feel if we lower our own fluency in what is our native language that we are somehow being good language hosts?

"Yes, we go to Roppongi," Larry added. "We do night life," he added with a giggle.

"This no Roppongi," the officer said. "This, this," and he struggled for the right word until one of his colleagues said palace, and he said, "This palace."

"Where Roppongi?" I said.

"This no Roppongi," he said.

"I see. No Roppongi. Where Roppongi?" I asked.

"Yes," Larry added, feeling compelled to voice his concerns: "Roppongi we go. Roppongi where?"

The man conferred with his colleagues and then repeated his earlier conclusion: "This no Roppongi. Roppongi not here."

"Not here," I said. "Where is here?"

"Here is palace," Larry said. "That is where here is."

The man looked at Larry and as if in confirmation of his own conclusion, said, "Yes. Here is palace. Now, you follow me."

I began to get off the bike, but the man put his hand on my shoulder. "No. You follow me motorcycle."

"Yes," I said.

73

The man walked across the street and got in his police car. He rolled down the window. "You follow," he said. Then he turned on his rooftop flashing light.

"We're going to fucking prison," Larry said.

"Could be," I said. I put it into gear and followed the police car out of the gate. His siren came on loud and shrill ripping the otherwise still Sunday night.

We followed him for twenty minutes or so, and it was then I turned and said to Larry, "I think he is taking us to Roppongi."

"A police escort for two drunk Americans," he said. "Fucking incredible."

And it was. We followed the car with its flashing lights and screaming siren through the labyrinthine streets until we arrived in Roppongi, the neon signs and foot traffic of late night revelers telling us we had arrived. We pulled up next to our escort. Through his open window, he said, "This Roppongi. Be careful."

"Thank you very much, sir," I said.

"Be careful," he said and drove off leaving us to choose our way among the hundreds of clubs that beckoned with both barkers and explosions of neon that rent the night air.

•

Etsuko and I are in the kitchen making crab cakes as her parents are preparing themselves for dinner. Gunnar and Karla should be arriving any minute.

"I think your father enjoyed the crabbing, don't you think?" I ask. We are sitting across the kitchen table from one another, each forming round cakes and patting them in the bowl of the cornmeal mixture. I have mixed the crab with a little mayonnaise, Dijon mustard, Worcestershire sauce, salt, pepper, lemon juice, three pieces of ground white bread, diced green onion, a pinch of baking powder and then the requisite chili powder. I have already prepared a Remoulade sauce to go

74

with the cakes.

"He had a wonderful time, Jake. I heard him talking with Mother about it."

"Good."

"You're sweet. And smart."

"What? Well, thank you, my dear. And you, too are smart and sweet."

She takes a sip of beer from her glass and leaves five prints of corn meal. "I meant that it was smart and sweet of you to have Father pull in the pots. To make him feel needed."

"Hell. I didn't want to blister up my fingers on that gnarly old rope." I take a sip of my own beer. I know what she means, but ward off the compliment. She comes around the table, takes my cheeks in each of her grimy hands, and kisses me on the lips.

"I love you," she says.

"And I love you who is the laziest daughter in all of Gumma. Remember?"

She laughs and sits back down on her side of the table. "Of course I remember," she says. "That was the day you fell in love with my mother."

"And if not for you, I would have married her."

"And if not for my father."

"That's what you said at the time."

We are each quiet and we carry on with our work. I am mired in the past, thinking of that day when I first met her family, and I think that she might be, too. I look up at her and I see tears running down each cheek. "I hope those are the tears of happiness, Etsuko."

She wipes each cheek with her sleeves. "Yes, Jake. They certainly are. It is just so good to have my parents here. The older they get, the more I worry about them."

The doorbell rings. Bacchus gets up from under the table and runs in place for a second before her feet take grip of the tiled floor and then she shoots out to the front door.

I leave Etsuko with the cakes, and I open the door to Gunnar and Karla who come into the entry hall, the dusk falling behind them. Bacchus waggles her entire body at their feet as they remove their shoes, and she gets a good rub from each as I take their coats.

Back in the kitchen, Gunnar and Karla join Etsuko in making crab cakes at the table as I make drinks. Lemon Drops for Karla and Etsuko, and heavy glasses of Scotch on the rocks for Gunnar and me. I deliver the glasses and we each drink.

"What a day, eh, Jake? It was like spring here," Gunnar says.

"It was beautiful at the coast," Etsuko says. "Warm and no wind."

"How was the crabbing?" Karla asks. "Did your parents enjoy it?"

"They did. Jake worked my father very hard."

"His hands are raw," I said. "But he seemed to like it."

"How many crab?" Gunnar asks.

"Twelve. And we got four dozen live oysters." I look at Karla and wink lewdly. "It's going to be some night."

She turns and smiles at Gunnar and I feel the warmth of their love.

Mother comes into the kitchen and Etsuko stands and in Japanese introduces both Karla and Gunnar who stand and return her bow. "Konbanwa," they both say and she, too, wishes them a good evening. Etsuko tells her to sit at the table and now she is engaged in making crab cakes with the rest of us just as Father comes in and everyone stands and Karla and Gunnar bow as does father.

Gunnar, Father and I go out to the patio where I've left the cooler and we show Father how to shuck oysters. I have two dozen of the petite Kumamotos and two dozen of the slightly larger Yaquinas. I shuck a Kumamoto and slurp it from its shell. Ah, the briny taste takes me back to the sea. Father grapples in an initial struggle, but then he finds the right place to twist the knife and the oyster pops open. He, too, takes his in a loud slurp and a smile spreads across his face.

Gunnar asks me to ask him how it was. "*Totemo oishii,*" he says. "A very good oyster. Yes, very good."

We sit around the picnic table with the porch light on, and we shuck all the Kumamotos leaving them embedded in their juices on the half shell, and it takes great strength to ignore these little fellows as we wait for the Yaquinas which are on the barbecue that is now smoking its mesquite aroma so that I am as hungry as it is possible to be. Mark Twain said that the first man to eat an oyster was a brave man indeed, and that may have been true. But once he ate one, he must have forgotten all about his daring for *ostrea virginica* must have left him palpably entranced.

We are at table. We pass the plates of crab cakes and raw and cooked oysters and bottles of Pinot gris and Pinot noir–Father has fallen somewhat in love with the latter while Mother seems smitten with the former, and for two people who do not, as a rule, drink alcohol, they are close to fouling out–and we eat and talk in general revelry as Etsuko translates back and forth.

"What did you think when Etsuko told you she was going to marry an American?" Karla asks Mother who waits for the translation.

Upon hearing the question in Japanese, she laughs with her hand politely before her mouth, but I can still see the flash of gold. She looks from Karla to me, and back to her daughter before laughing again. "With Etsuko, nothing ever surprises me," she says.

"But did you think it a bad thing?" Karla presses.

"Bad?"

Etsuko is going back and forth between English and Japanese so that the room is spinning with language.

"Well, were you against it?" Karla asks forcing Etsuko to ask her own mother if she disapproved of her own marriage with her own husband looking on.

"I wasn't terribly for it," she says which Etsuko says, and I laugh now hearing Etsuko say she wasn't terribly for marrying me, and then mother looks at me, smiles and says, "But now I am for it, yes, Jake-san is," and she takes a sip of wine and I wonder if Etsuko will do so, too, in translating the gesture, "a funny man."

This so surprises me when I first hear Mother say this and then Etsuko that I choke on my wine and then fall into laughter, coughing all the while as Gunnar, sitting next to me, pounds me on the back with a great enthusiasm for now he is laughing as well. Stoic Father watches all this with a bemused gaze that seems to confirm Mother's assessment of me.

"And what about you?" Karla asks as she looks at Father. "What did you think?"

Father takes a small sip of wine and sets down his glass. "I think," he says, "that any man who can present us with a meal as fine as this is a good man and a good husband."

In translating this, Etsuko looks at me and I tell Father thank you, and then I say, "And thank you for having such a wonderful daughter as Etsuko," and I smile at her, then wink.

"The laziest daughter in all of Japan," Mother says as she first laughs and then blushes.

"What did she say?" Karla asks.

"That I am the laziest daughter in all of Japan."

"Why would she say that?" Karla wants to know.

"Just an old joke, Karla," I tell her through clouds of my own laughter.

We sit at the table eating and drinking as the night falls away. Gunnar is interested in Father's farm where he grows rice and when he tells Gunnar that he also raises silk worms, Gunnar is wild with questions in sincere interest. "There is a festival next month in Nagano Prefecture," Etsuko translates, "where there is much sericulture. The Hatsu-uma festival is a celebration of the god of silk worms, O-shira-sama."

Father pauses which allows Etsuko to take a bite of crab cake. "These are delicious," she says with a mouthful.

"Tell us about the God of silkworms," Gunnar says. Then:

"Sorry, Etsuko."

"No worries," she says. It is her fondest Australian expression. We once spent a December in Queensland.

Etsuko asks her father to tell us about the god of silkworms. He takes another sip of wine. Mother sits next to him waiting for a story as she has done all her life. Father does love a captive audience and he has one in us. Karla, too, is interested in what he has to say. He speaks and Etsuko speaks and together they weave this story:

"One time so long ago as to hardly be remembered, the young daughter of a wealthy family fell in love with a beautiful and magnificent horse that they kept in a corral. When her father learned of this affair, he went into a rage and killed the horse. In the greatest of despairs when there is no such thing as hope, the girl became ill and died.

"The spirits of both the horse and the girl found themselves together in heaven, but soon they descended to earth and when they landed on the mulberry bush in the garden, they transformed into silkworms."

"That's a great story," Gunnar says.

"From this," Etsuko says, "we have dolls called O-Shira-sama. They are made from mulberry sticks. O-Shira-sama is also the guardian of children."

"You've seen my kimono?" I say. "Mother made that for me from their very own silk."

"Really?" Gunnar says. "That's incredible."

"I've never seen it," Karla says. "Go put it on for me."

"Really?" I say.

"Go," she says. "I want to see it." Karla is used to having her way.

"Alright. Just a minute."

I get up and leave the table. Bacchus follows me to the bedroom. I go into the closet where the kimono hangs and I put it on. It is smooth to the skin, glassy and sleek. I tie the obi and I put on wooden geta and I walk back out to the dining room where Mother is using her hands to tell Gunnar and Karla about weaving, and it is as if I have arrived on cue

79

for she takes a hold of my arm and points to various parts of my kimono in her explanation of her fine art.

"You know what you ought to do?" Karla asks the entire table as if her thoughts are still being formed and her audience is as yet undetermined.

"What's that, Karla?" I step in.

"I mean if you really are set in having those three punks for dinner?"

"Yes," Etsuko says.

"Well, have them wear kimonos."

"Why?" I say.

"Well, it would be one more step in getting them to be someone who they are not."

"Good, Karla," Gunnar says. "But where will they get the extra kimonos?"

"I have just one," Etsuko says. "And Jake has just one. I plan to wear it that evening."

"We don't even know if the judge will agree to this crazy plan," I say.

Karla smiles. "Your mother. She can make them."

"What?"

"And I could help. I would love to learn from her."

Etsuko looks at Karla as if she has just announced her own admittance to the state mental hospital. "Come on, Etsuko," Karla says. "Think how much fun the three of us would have."

"I don't even have a loom."

"You don't need one. We'll buy bolts of silk."

Karla had taken over as she so often has done in the past. After initial hesitation, even mother is excited as she tells the women what they will need to get started. Thus, we have our coffee and Calvados in separate camps. Mother, Etsuko and Karla at the dining table discussing what they will need to get started; Father, Gunnar and I by the fireplace discussing haiku.

•

Etsuko was none too pleased when I returned from Roppongi Monday morning as she was leaving for work, but going into our marriage she knew full well that upon occasion I would get a wild hair which I would inevitably scratch. One sweltry night the summer before, Larry and I had been drinking at Bonards when I suggested we cool off by swimming in the Edo River, a festering mass of debris that separated Ichikawa from Tokyo. We stripped down, left our clothes on the rocks and swam through the flotsam. When we arrived on the other side of the river, the sun was just coming up. As we stood up in the shallows, we noticed an old man sitting on a rock with a fishing pole in hand. When he saw us–two naked *gaijins*–his eyes went wide and his jaw dropped. He quickly reeled in and trotted off up the shore maybe thinking we had followed his bait until we stood just before him, two foreign apparitions up to no good.

In August the year of our marriage, Etsuko and I decided we had better climb Mt. Fuji, for it is something everyone must do once in her life, she told me, and though she had worked at a lodge on the mountain one summer when she was in college, she had never made the climb.

It was five in the evening when we started the climb at what is known as the Fifth Station which is largely a tourist trap replete with myriad Fuji-san memorabilia including walking sticks adorned with both the Japanese Flag and small bells. We took the bells off our sticks so as not to draw attention to ourselves, but as we began the climb I heard that few of the hundreds of other climbers above us were similarly inclined: the cool, dusk air tinkled with their progress up the steep and serpentine trail.

"You worked here three months and you never climbed to the top?"

Etsuko stopped and turned to look back at me. "I was busy," she said before turning to resume our climb.

"Busy," I said. "Busy." I laughed. "Etsuko was busy."

It was the gloaming and dusk was slipping to night, and as it grew darker, the climbers before us and those behind us turned on their flashlights so that under this night of stars it appeared there was a very long and sinuous snake slithering up Mt. Fuji, Japan's most sacred mountain, and we were part of it as it wound up the switchbacks of the rocky trail.

At the Sixth Station, we stopped to have our walking sticks branded for the price of one-hundred yen as did the other climbers at each station so that they could return home with proof of their ascent. After waiting in line for ten minutes, we had the brand burned into our sticks, and we moved on. It was ten in the evening when we stopped at the Seventh Station where, after paying for another brand, we entered the small lodge and sat down by the fire. Here we would eat a meal and then sleep for four hours before resuming our climb to the summit where, if we timed it right, we would see the sun rise.

The night air had at first been refreshing after the heat and humidity of a Tokyo August, but then it became down right cold and the warmth of the fire was soporific. We ate *onigiri*–rice balls filled with salmon and wrapped in crisp, green seaweed–and drank Sapporo beer as other climbers came and went in the smoky room where the fire burned in an open pit.

"So, three months here, Etsuko? And you never climbed the mountain?"

"No, Jake. But I am climbing it now. And with you, a *gaijin*, no less."

"With blond hair and blue eyes."

"Yes."

"Why is it so important that everyone make this trek?" I took a bite of the *onigiri* and chased it with cold beer. Ah, beer is a beverage of the gods. Nothing like a lager after a physical workout, and we had been climbing almost five hours. I could feel the trek in my thighs. But beer, beer, she revived me and made the world seem right.

"It is just that this is our most sacred mountain." Etsuko finished eating and drank from her own glass of beer.

"But why?"

"There are many legends. One has it that it is our oldest mountain and that it arose in a single night. An old woodsman heard an explosion and as he came out of his hut, he saw the mountain rise up out of the Suruga plains. Fire shot out of the top of the mountain, and this man named it Fuji."

"Why?"

"That means never die. Anyway, soon after he witnessed this event, he was visited by an old priest who asked him if he prayed. He said that no, with his family and his work, he was far too busy to pray. Well, the priest told him of hell and said that he would go there in the form of a toad unless he prayed and this so scared the man that that is all he did. Pray, pray, pray."

"And what, Etsuko darling, happened, pray tell?"

"Funny, Jake. His wife was angry with him for he did not work. She was after him day and night, but all he did was pray. Finally, he could not take it anymore and he climbed up Mt. Fuji where he stayed for three hundred years. It is said that when there is a full moon, his spirit haunts the mountain."

"Is there more?"

"More?"

"About him."

"Not that I know of."

We were silent now as I thought of the old woodsman, the Japanese Rip Van Winkle. "Who are all these people wearing white?" It seemed that half the people climbing were dressed in white garb.

"Ah, those are the Fuji-ko. They worship the mountain and believe the peak is the beginning of heaven and earth. They make this climb every year. I think the pilgrimage began in the sixteen century."

After some time, a man came and led us to the back room which resembled a morgue in that the walls were lined with platforms, three high, where we were to lie down and sleep for a few hours before resuming our climb. I lay next to Etsuko and listened to the sounds of snoring and sighing.

"Etsuko," I whispered.

"What?" She whispered back.

"Let's make love."

She pushed my hand away from her breast. "Are you crazy?"

"No. I thought it would be good to make love on this, the most sacred mountain in Japan. Our own little ritual."

"You are crazy. Now go to sleep."

She drifted off, and I lay there wishing that we could fall asleep together so that we could be unified in one dream.

After two cups of green tea, we were back out in the cold under a sky of stars. A cloud passed over and spilled its rain, and then the breeze carried it on. The night was a tinkling of bells so that this did seem somehow sacred. We passed old women resting on rocks and families with small children as well. It did not seem that we were walking individually; rather, it seemed we were part of something much bigger, this long and twisting chain of white light a pilgrimage.

We arrived at the summit before sunrise, bought cups of green tea from a shop and found a place to relax while we waited. And then the sun rose from the only cloud on the horizon. The orange light first reached out across Sagami Bay and then spread to the trees and lakes beneath us. "Etusko," I said with my arms around her shoulders. "I love you."

•

The memoir progresses apace, neither fast nor slow. I finished writing about climbing Mt. Fuji this morning as Bacchus lay at my feet. I wonder now how well a dog remembers, how far back she can recall. Does she, for example, even remember swimming after that goose a few weeks back, or is it that she is merely in the here and now?

"Well, Bacchus," I say and she stands when she hears her name. "Let's go find out what everyone is doing."

In the family room with the view of the hills that rise above our back yard, I find the three women at work unpacking the silk they have purchased. "How did it go?" Etsuko asks me referring to my morning's writing session.

"Well enough," I say. "It was your first ascent of Mt. Fuji. You were tired, and I had to carry you on my back."

"Ha, ha. You think you're funny."

"You climbed Mt. Fuji?" Karla asks from her knees as she spreads out a bolt of gray silk. Mother sits in an easy chair watching the two younger women who are on their knees.

"We did," Etsuko says.

"Tell me about it," Karla says. "Was it difficult?"

"Not really."

"We have to leave in an hour," I interupt. "Where's Father?"

"On a walk to the pond," Etsuko says.

"I'll go find him," I say. "Come on, Bacchus."

As I leave the room, I hear Etsuko say, "Jake was a bit slow, but I helped him to the summit," and I find myself smiling again. If only we could bottle up my happy memories, we could offer them to those who are clinically depressed. I know just a teaspoon or two would pick them up out of their doldrums better than any Prozac or whatever the latest happy pill is we find advertised on nightly television, those commercials always armed with warnings of possible side effects such as explosions of the various internal organs. *This pill will make you happy, but in certain situations it is possible that your liver may be jettisoned in a bowel movement. If this occurs, see your doctor immediately.*

We go out into the cold breeze, Bacchus running ahead with her nose up in the air taking in all the smells in the world. I wonder if she has a system for classifying these smells, if she can sort them and file them away where they will be joined by others so that any memory she has will be entirely comprised of entwined redolence. Or, it may be that each new scent dislodges that which was previous so that the current smell is all that there is, and thus there is contentment. What a sad world for a dog if she were to live inside a bubble devoid of the olfactory. As I now walk down the path toward the pond, I think what strange thoughts occur to me! It may be I am trying to avoid that which maybe should be on my mind: this afternoon's sentencing hearing where we will once again encounter the three punks whom Etsuko wishes to rehabilitate by inviting them to dinner.

I see Father skipping stones on the pond. Bacchus runs up to him and nuzzles his crotch. Father bends down and pets Bacchus behind the ears. "*Konnichi-wa, oto-san*," I say. "How are you this morning?"

"*Genki-des.*"

He seems embarrassed at having been caught skipping rocks, so I bend down and choose three or four relatively flat rocks. "Bacchus, stay," I say for I know she will follow the rock into the pond, retriever that she is. She once followed a seagull into the shipping lanes of the Columbia River as I hollered for her to *come, come, come,* but she was obsessed with that bird and I am convinced that if the bird had not banked back toward the south shore where I stood, Bacchus would now be somewhere in Northern Canada.

I skip the stone and watch it bounce five times before sinking out of sight.

"*Jyozu-desu,*" Father says. Very good.

"*Goma-suri desu ne,*" I reply. Sesame seed grinding is the literal translation, meaning you are flattering me. Etymology? I haven't a clue.

He picks up a stone and skips it seven times across the water. I try again and make it six. Father, nine. Me, eight. Father, seven. Me, five. Bacchus watches us release the stones, and then follows them with her head wishing she could bounce into the water after them. As we throw the stones, Father asks me about Elin.

"She'll be coming home next week" I tell him. "She is looking forward to seeing you."

"Etsuko says she is good at basketball." He skips one eleven times. I congratulate him.

"Yes. In fact, tomorrow we can watch. Her game will be on t.v."

Father smiles at this. He is stoic, but he cannot hide his love for and his pride in his only granddaughter.

Bacchus tires of watching us throw rocks and she leaps into the air after a rock Father has thrown. She crashes into the water with a huge splash just as the rock makes its sixth or seventh gambol, Bacchus swimming fiercely in its direction, and she slows and treads water where it sank, looking in every direction for the lost stone.

"Bacchus," I yell in a tone Father can recognize as anger. "Get back here." Which of course is the wrong thing to say for Bacchus comes bounding back through the water. She runs up to father and shakes off as much of it as she can. He laughs. "Bacchus, god damn it," I say. She shakes off again and we turn to walk up toward the house.

"Jake-san," Father says. "One should always be kind to dogs."

"I know. I was just angry because she disobeyed." It starts to rain now, a slight drizzle.

"We had a law that said you had to be kind to dogs at risk of being sent into exile." Father walks with his hands behind his back and I find myself doing the same.

As we walk slowly up the path toward the house, he tells me of the fifth Tokugawa shogun in 1687 who, because he had been born in the year of the dog, commanded the people to be kind to dogs. Under this law, many people were sentenced to death for beating or killing dogs. Stray dogs were gathered together at a pound in Okubo which, it was said, housed over 100,000 dogs. To meet the huge burden of feeding these animals, a dog tax was enacted so that every district in the country had to pay this tax with rice.

"What a great time to be a dog," I say.

"Yes," Father replies. "But when Tsunayoshi died, the law was rescinded and some 12,000 people were released from jail."

We have arrived in the driveway. Bacchus is already in the

garage waiting to be wiped down.

"What happened to all of the dogs in the pound?" I ask.

"That I do not know. But the people were happy."

We go into the garage and I pull down a towel from a hook on the wall. I rub Bacchus dry as father watches. As we go inside to the trio of women, he says, "Bacchus has a lovely life."

I smile and silently agree.

•

Etsuko finished making *onigiri* and I put two bottles of sake in the basket with the beer. It was a warm Sunday morning in mid-April and we were going to Ueno Park in Tokyo for *Hanami*, literally cherry blossom viewing. *Hanami* is celebrated by everyone in Japan by eating and drinking under a blossoming cherry tree of which there are hundreds of varieties. Etsuko told me that the celebration started more than fifteen centuries prior, but only the aristocrats were afforded the luxury of the event.

"When were plebeians like us allowed such pleasures?" I asked her as I put on my shoes in the entry way.

"Plebeians?" She asked as she loaded a basket with food for our picnic.

"Commoners, dear."

"Some three hundred years ago." She closed the basket. "I am ready to go."

"How do you know such esoterica?"

"Japanese history. I was a very good student."

"Of that I have no doubt."

She joined me in the entry way and put on her shoes. We were off, each carrying a large picnic basket. We walked out of the shadow of our apartment building and into the sun of Daimon Dori. We walked down the narrow lane toward the train station as shop keepers pulled up their aluminum doors. Men and women busied themselves in the sun by sweeping the street before their shops. We exchanged greetings with these people where we shopped each day. It gave me a warm feeling to share the commerce of their smiles. We passed Bonards, and I asked if we should see if Toshichan were home.

"He'll have left already," Etsuko said. "He wanted to be there early to find a good tree."

On the train, we set the baskets on the seat next to us and enjoyed the luxury of weekend lassitude. On a weekday, we would be standing squeezed in by other bodies, but today the train was relatively empty.

We alighted at Ueno Station and made our way through the crowd of *Ameyokocho*, a bustling market beneath the elevated train tracks. At Ueno Park, we climbed the steps and meandered along the paths looking for our group of friends. Already, the park was crowded with revelers sitting on blankets beneath canopies of pink and white blossoms. There was music and singing and dancing and it was not yet ten in the morning.

A man came toward us along the pathway in a clumsy state of inebriation. He stopped directly in front of us as if to not allow us to pass. "*Ohayo gozaimus, gaijin-san,*" he slurred. When he bowed, I thought he was going to fall over, but he righted himself with a wobble and a hiccup.

I returned his greeting.

In English, he said, "You like Japan?"

"Yes, very much."

"You like cherry tree?"

"Yes, I do."

"You like *Hanami*?"

"Yes. It is a wonderful custom."

"Let's go Jake," Etsuko said, her free arm tugging mine.

"Wait," the drunk said and from a sack he withdrew a pint of Suntory whiskey. "Have drink."

I took the proffered bottle and drank. I smiled and thanked

him. "You have good time," he said and then he continued past us along the path.

"He was an amiable sort," I said.

"Drunk as a monkey," Etsuko said employing another idiom she had heard me say. I enjoyed hearing my own idioms roll off her tongue, especially when she mixed them together so that very little could be made of them. Only two nights before, Etsuko lay on the futon waiting for me to climb in, and she yawned and said, "I'm tits up," to which I responded, "And I'm sure glad you are."

We saw Toshichan and his wife Takako and several other of our friends, both Japanese and American, sitting on blankets beneath a huge Sakura tree laden with pink flowers. A slight breeze, a warm caress, rustled the branches and blossoms floated on the perfumed air. I squeezed Etsuko's arm as we approached and said, "This is a rich life," and she said, "Rich as rain." I laughed at that one, too.

"No, Etsuko. It's right as rain," but before I could explain we were busy being greeted by our friends, many of whom were well on their way to being happily drunk. We spread out our dishes of food with the others, and sat down with everyone.

It was a glorious day with the warmth of the sun filtering through pink flowers. There were twenty or twenty-five of us and each had brought several dishes so that we had a literal smorgasbord laid out before us: *onigiri, sashimi, sushi, satsuma-imo, oden, sembei, Sunomono, otsumami* and more. There were several kinds of beer, Sapporo, Kirin, Asahi, and bottles of sake the labels of which I could not read. There were several kinds of whiskey as well.

We ate and drank and sang songs and traded stories throughout the day until the long shadows brought in the cool of the spring evening. Etsuko and I were among the first to leave. Compared to many of the others, we were quite sober. We rode the train home with empty baskets and we walked back up Daimon Dori in the dark.

As we crawled into bed, I said, "That was quite a day."

"I love *Hanami*," Etsuko said.

"Did you have *Hanami* when you were a little girl?"

"Of course. My grandmother would cook for two days before our picnic and we would eat all day. At night my father would light lanterns and we would stay out until midnight."

I rolled onto my side and cupped a breast. "You're tits up tonight," I said.

"Not really. Just a little," she said.

"Oh, but you're wrong. You really are tits up." To prove my point I pulled back the covers and kissed her breasts. "See what I mean?"

She said she did as she reached and turned off the light.

•

We sit in the front row of the courtroom, and sitting here reminds me of the Lutheran church I attended when I was a boy: the hard wooden pew, slick as ice; the quiet air of expectation, the somber wait; the judge's mien as serious as any priest's. Etsuko sits on the aisle wearing the kimono her mother made her when she graduated high school; I sit next to her, then Father and Mother. Father wears a navy blue suit with white shirt and tie while Mother wears a gray and silver kimono. I feel under-dressed in pressed Levis with a new denim shirt and brown tweed jacket, but then I have no intention of dressing up for the sentencing of three skinheads.

I stare at the three of them sitting there next to their defense attorney. All three of them have cleanly shaven heads. They wear tee shirts and jeans and Doc Martins and sitting there next to the man in a suit, they look dangerous and mean like some kind of feral animal that has been caught and temporarily caged. It is absolutely ludicrous what Etsuko is about to do, I think, but she is as determined as any righteous warrior. She epitomizes this from the Tao: *The sage has no mind of his own./He is aware of the needs of others./ I am good to people who are good./ I am also good to people who are not good./ Because virtue is goodness./ I have faith in people who are faithful./ I also have faith in people who are not faithful./ Because virtue is faithfulness./ The sage is shy and humble-to the world he seems confusing./ Men look to him and listen./ He behaves like a little child.*

After some preliminary discussion between the prosecutor, the defense attorney and the judge, the judge, who has a chiseled face beneath brown bangs, says, "Ms. Etsuko Weedsong, I believe you had something you wanted to say before I determine the sentence for the three defendants."

Etsuko stands up. "Yes, your honor." From where I sit, she looks tall in the wooden geta she wears on her feet.

"You agree with the prosecution in wishing for the maximum sentence for all three defendants, I assume," the judge says. She looks from Etsuko to the prosecutor who is sitting behind a table.

"No, your honor."

"Well, what is it you wish to tell the court?" The judge pulls the sleeve of her robe back and looks at her watch.

"Sending these men to prison will not do any good."

"In this country, when someone commits a crime and is found guilty, he is punished, Ms. Weedsong."

"Yes, I know."

"Well, what would you suggest?"

"I would like all three men to be sentenced to having dinner at our house," Etsuko says.

The judge lets out a quick, short laugh and says, "You're that bad a cook?"

"No, it's..."

"You plan to poison them then?"

I think of a dinner of tainted *fugu* now prepared by a chef whose license has been revoked because of sloppy slicing.

"No. You miss the point."

The judge frowns, grows serious. "And what is the point?"

Etsuko takes a deep breath. She walks before the defendants and looks each full in the face. Then she turns back to the judge.

"Prison will not cure these young men of racism. In fact, prison will make them worse than they already are. For whatever reason, all three men are racist, yet I doubt that any of them has ever been to another country. They know nothing of other people's customs. It is my belief that communication can resolve any problem, and I would like to communicate to these young men through interaction over a meal."

"A rather naive belief," the judge says.

"Maybe so. But you have to admit that prison will not help them overcome racism."

"True."

"And hate."

"Yes, you have a point."

"I propose that they become different people for an evening. That might also help them understand who they are."

The judge looks to the court-appointed defense attorney. "Do you have any objections, Mr. Wiedeman?"

He frowns. "No, none at all."

"And you, Ms. Wangen?" She looks to the prosecutor.

"Well, this is a hate crime. It is a bit of a light sentence."

"True," says the judge.

"It was a hate crime against me," Etsuko says. "And I would like to try to eradicate the hate."

"I don't know that that can be done," the judge says and sighs.

"But prison will only make them worse."

"Who will be at the dinner?"

"My mother and father here," she says as she looks at her parents. "Jake. Our daughter Elin. Two friends."

"I see," says the judge. "And you think this will somehow change them?"

"I don't know. But they aren't going to learn to empathize in jail."

The judge is quiet now. She is looking at the defendants. "Okay, then," she says. "I hereby sentence you, Daniel Dunn, and you,

Leonard Harmon, and you, Keegan Porter, to dinner at Jake and Etsuko Weedsong's house on," she turns to look at Etsuko, "When?"

"Next Friday?"

"On Friday, February 2, from 6 p.m. to 10 p.m."

"Your honor?" Etsuko says.

"Yes?"

"My mother–that's her sitting next to my father–is going to make kimonos for the three of them to wear. I'm making a traditional Japanese dinner."

"What are you having?"

"Among other things, *te-maki* sushi."

"I ain't eating no raw fish," the young man named Daniel Dunn says. He is good looking young man with wide, powerful shoulders. He is tall and strong with an athletic build. Nothing about him looks happy. He looks ready to bite through a two-by-four. I remember him as being the one who first accosted us, who first knocked me down with a blow to my jaw that sent me reeling.

The judge gives him a savage look. "You will eat everything put before you," and then to the bailiff: "Milton, are you free Friday?"

"Yes I am." The bailiff is a huge black man, maybe six feet six inches tall, rippling with muscle. He has not once smiled in this court room, and I wonder if he hangs his smiles at home before he leaves for the day.

"Would you please attend the dinner?"

"Yes, your honor. I would be happy to."

"And make sure these boys behave properly."

"It would be my pleasure." Still, no revealing of emotion.

"Because if they don't, they will be back here in this court to be re-sentenced." She turns her look to the defense attorney. "One more outburst by any of the defendants, and I will find them in contempt of court."

"Yes, your honor," Mr. Wiedeman says.

"Your honor?" Etsuko says.

"Yes?"

"The kimonos? My mother needs to take measurements now."

"Of course."

Etsuko tells her mother to come with her and the two women approach the table behind which the defendants sit.

"Stand up," the judge says.

The three boys stand up. Mother bows to the first one–Keegan Porter, the youngest–and he stands at attention as Mother works him over with a tape measure as Etsuko writes down the measurements she is told. I find this scene both amusing and disturbing as my wife and my mother-in-law measure these men who hate them so–amusing in that Mother is being so polite to them who would possibly kill her daughter, and disturbing for the same reason. This boy looks nervous, his small frame stiff as a board under the measuring tape. His Adam's Apple goes up and down as he swallows his nerves. He cannot weigh more than 150 pounds. His hair is also closely cropped, but I can detect the red hue of it that goes along with his ruddy cheeks that blush now as one Japanese woman measures him, her daughter jotting everything down. He is eighteen years old and still has a field of acne. If he had something to say now, I wonder what it would be.

The judge, the prosecutor, the bailiff, the defense attorney, Father, me: We all watch in silence. And I wonder: Is it possible to reform and refine these men, to transform them like butterflies from cocoons? Can we, through education, cure these boys of hate?

They move to Daniel Dunn, measuring his six foot frame. He stands as if at attention, his jaw held high, his eyes staring straight at the wall before him, not in any way acknowledging the two women. This young man's posture is perfect. He looks to be eighteen, nineteen, or twenty, possibly the oldest of the three, but that may only because his bearing makes him appear as the leader.

Then they move to the large man, Leonard Harmon, and he is bigger than Dunn but not as big as the bailiff. He wears a slow, clumsy smile as if he is not quite sure how he is supposed to react to being measured for a kimono, a garment he may not ever have heard of before.

He tries to stand straight like Dunn, but his shoulders are hunched, and it is as if his spine were made of rubber. As they finish, Harmon says, "Thank you," before he realizes his mistake, and Dunn turns his head and glares at him. Harmon just shrugs his shoulders and smiles dumbly as if he didn't know enough not to thank them for taking the time to measure his large and unruly frame.

I smile now as I see the earnest look in Etsuko's whole demeanor, and I feel lucky to love her.

And then I think: Next Friday we're having three skinheads over to dinner. That'll be a treat.

The next morning I am up before anyone else. Bacchus follows me into the kitchen where I make coffee. I let her out the back door and she trots out into the rainy dawn and walks around the lawn with her nose to the ground, snorting for the proper place to pee. Finally, she finds her favorite spot and squats to pee. I watch and she does what I do not want her to do: with her hind legs, she kicks up the grass to spread her scent in self-aggrandizing advertisement; it doesn't matter to her that the nearest dog is a half mile away. As she rips up the lawn with her sharp claws, I hiss *no* but not loud enough for her to hear for I don't want to wake the others. Bacchus trots back to the door with her nose held high, inhaling the morning smells. She acts unaware of her transgression, but I believe she knows what she did. "Bacchus," I whisper as I wipe her paws with an old towel that hangs on a hook by the door just for this purpose, "you're a little whore." At this she wags her tail, and I scratch her neck.

I've made a pot of coffee and I sit here in my study with Bacchus at my feet. I enjoyed writing of Hanami yesterday, and now I mull over where it is I am to go in this act of remembrance. The Tao says, *"He who stands on tiptoe is not steady./He who strides cannot maintain pace./He who makes a show is not enlightened./He who is self-righteous is not respected./He who boasts achieves nothing./He who brags will not endure." According to the followers of the Tao, "These are extra food and* unnecessary luggage."/*They do not bring happiness./Therefore followers of the Tao avoid them.*"

So, maybe it is that I am not ready to write this memoir? For it is true that I am making an effort to remember what happens next. Is the Tao, then, wrong? But then, the very word *next* is what confounds for our memories do not arrive in the present in any chronological order. They are recalled when a catalyst triggers them from the past into the present so that the two commingle in a colonization of time. What I do today is greatly affected by the intrusion of memory so that each of our lives is a memoir being constantly unfolded for what is the opposite of now? The answer, of course, is that there is no answer. As I write this I recall Borges' brilliant short story "The Garden of Forking Paths," that great riddle on the nature of time. If I were young and starting over, I would study physics because the answer to everything lies in space; each religion helps us avoid the arduous trek for truth with a suggestion of a higher being, something I find sad but amusing in that each considers its own God superlative to all others.

So what is the catalyst for my now remembering our trip to Hiroshima? My now is sitting here at this desk with Bacchus snoring, the cold winter rain slapping the window of my study as Etsuko and her parents sleep through this dark Saturday morning, tucked in by Morpheus and warmly ensconced in their separate dreams.

•

Hiroshima. That is where Etsuko and I went during the school break a couple of weeks after celebrating *Hanami* with our friends in Ueno. I had always wanted to go for various reasons, chief among them that Hiroshima was the city where the course of history was forever changed not unlike a river dammed and diverted. Once we realized that thousands of people could be killed at the same time without warning, killed by a bomb dropped from the sky, we were no longer safe with our naive notion that there was such a thing as immunity from the will of others. Although the bomb certainly shortened the war, and may have saved lives in the long run, humankind would be far better off had the bomb never been invented for it is surely to be the cause of our ultimate and entire demise.

We stayed at a small *minshuku* a few blocks from the epicenter. We had arrived late the evening before, and we woke late, the sun blazing through the *shoji*, warming my face where I lay next to Etsuko on the futon. I had a strange feeling lying there, and then this conscious thought: I am American, I thought. I have come to the city where we dropped an atom bomb on the morning of August 6th, a morning when little boys and little girls were walking to school. What must they have thought before they died? That the world was coming to an end? What did their mothers think as they cleaned the morning dishes? Were their children safe? And what did their fathers think? Were their wives still at home?

As I lay there, warmed by the sun, Etsuko sleeping next to me, I felt some guilt. Not for being American. But for being human. And then I thought that maybe that was a healthy thing to feel for it would help me carry myself with less foolish pride.

Etsuko awoke. I turned and kissed her. "Good morning, Jake," she said. "How did you sleep?"

I told her fine and then I told her about what I had been mulling over this morning. "And then, for good measure, we dropped another bomb on Nagasaki three days later."

"I know, Jake. I know."

I propped myself on an elbow. "It pisses me off. Still."

"I know." She put her hand on my chest and pushed me back down on the futon. She crawled on top of me and rubbed my chest with both of her soft hands. "Let's not talk," she said. She leaned down and kissed me and I wrapped my arms around her back and we made love on a sunny morning in Hiroshima, our love an unconscious effort to cleanse the past. But then, I thought, not even love could do that.

We walked along the winding street to the shrine that was the epicenter. The cherry trees were mostly leafing out, but there were still scattered blossoms and their pink perfume carried on the air. Towering above everything in the park was a stone dome that was not fully destroyed by the blast. It had been a theater, and its roof was partially demolished. We stood and looked up at the structure and I found myself wondering if the men in the Enola Gay could have possibly known just what human folly they were engaged in, how they were players in the decision that ultimately there would be no future for the planet earth and its myriad inhabitants.

We walked through the park, each of us engaged in our separate thoughts. Little children ran in front of their parents, wild and filled with spring. Kimono-clad old women walked stooped over with osteoporosis, their hands clasped behind their backs. Everything save the children was solemn. As we walked, I thought that we stood at the center of the end of the world and that everyone should come here once and walk in silence just so as to know why someday there would be no more.

"Etsuko," I said. "What are you thinking?"

"I don't know, many things. I am thinking of my parents for one."

I took her hand and we walked in step. "Why your parents?"

"I don't know. Maybe it is because when I think of death, I think of them."

I thought about that and said nothing. We were content to be together in our so somber silence. We approached the museum and climbed up the steps, paid and went in, and we walked through the gallery of destruction, photos of burned-out land where once stood houses; pictures of children running, open-mouthed with terror; a girl with finger nails melted two inches long, her eyes stretched wide. We stayed inside this building for an hour and not once, never did we say a word. When we were back outside in the sunshine, we looked at each other and I bent down and kissed Etsuko and held her hands, and there on the steps above the park that was the epicenter of the blast of an American atomic bomb made in Los Alamos, New Mexico, I first trembled and then cried.

•

We are in the family room watching the basketball game, the four of us sitting around the *hori gotatsu* we had the builders add to the plans. I remember the contractor look at me as if I had a hole in my head and he was trying to figure out just how big a hole it was. "You want a hole in the floor?" he said as we stood in the mud as the foundation was being poured.

"Yes," I told him. "It's Japanese. You then put a heater at the bottom of it, place a small table called a *kotatsu* above it, and you sit at this table on winter nights, your legs warming as you drink hot sake. You'll see. You'll love it."

And he did. When the house was built and the tatami floors were installed in this room, I had him sit at the table with me, the blankets from the table draped over our laps, and after two bottle of sake he said, "Jake, this is some kind of invention." One some six hundred years old, the precursor of which was the *irori*, a sensible fire pit in the hearth room where a slow fired burned keeping the house warm and the iron kettle hanging above it full of hot water always ready for tea. Beneath the reed-thatched roofs of these old farm houses there was a gap to allow the smoke to exit beneath the eaves, and this, in turn, kept the roofs warm and dry and insect-free. Although there was a separate kitchen and the *irori* was not used to cook proper meals, children enjoyed placing sweet potatoes in the ashes over which they also warmed their rice cakes, but they had to be careful not to disturb the ashes with their feet for legend had it that if they did, it would cause the birds to destroy the rice fields. Today, it is around the kotatsu that family and guests gather to enjoy each other's company, just as they did long before around a slow burning fire.

This is my favorite room for it is an exact replica of Mother and

Father's, and it is a room where we do no work. We open the sliding shoji and look out upon the garden that is now white with newly fallen snow. The lights shine on the waterfall that fills our pond with oxygen so the koi can survive and it is a thing of beauty, this garden. In the summer, I sit and listen to the water fall and curl into itself, and back again through the rocks so that it circles and the sound purifies me.

I have opened the doors to the cupboard which hides our television for we do not wish it to be intrusive when it is not on. In graduate school, my writing instructor once said that the only reason we build houses is to keep our televisions out of the weather. We watch very little television. If a good drama appears–which is very, very rare–we will watch that. Other than that we watch sporting events and the news. I find it ironic that reality television is such a popular distraction from the reality of the viewers' lives.

Stanford is playing UCLA this evening. There are seven minutes left in the game, Stanford down by three, and Elin is bringing the ball up the court. She does a crossover at mid-court, goes from right to left, drives down the lane and gives a ball fake before going up for a lay-up. As she kisses the ball off the glass and into the cylinder, she is hammered to the floor by UCLA's center, and Mother shouts "*Gambatte, Elin-chan, gambatte.*"

Father slams his fist down on the table top so that I have to catch the bottle of sake before it tips over. Elin is still on the floor, players standing in a circle above her, the trainer working her knee. "That bitch," Etsuko says in English. "She hit her on purpose." I think, good thing we are not at the game or my dear and diminutive wife would be climbing over rows of spectators to get at the behemoth who knocked my little girl down to the floor.

"Easy, Etsuko," I say and take her hand.

We watch as the seconds slip by and still she lies on the floor. Then two players help her up by the arms and as she stands, as the crowd applauds, Mother says in Japanese, "That was a criminal offense. They should take her away in handcuffs."

I laugh. Elin goes to the line for the foul shot. I can see she is hurt as she limps, and I feel proud of her and I suppress the inevitable tears that wet my eyes with warmth, with love for this girl of mine who stands there on national t.v. readying to shoot the ball, the shot I taught her to take in our driveway all those years ago.

"*Gambatte, Elin-Chan*," Mother shouts now. "*Gambatte.*"

Elin bends her knees, spins the ball in her hands, dribbles five times, her torso rises from the waist, her knees extend, she rises to the balls of her feet, her wrists and elbows move forward, and she releases the ball. It sails up in a slow bending arc until it hits the back of the rim and bounces off the cylinder and into the hands of her teammate who puts it back off the glass for a four point play and the lead.

We all sigh in unison. Elin comes out of the game and we worry about the severity of her injury, but as it turns out it is minor for she is back in the game five minutes later and Stanford has won 67 to 61. Elin had seven points, eight assists, two rebounds and three steals. I write this down for I keep a journal of her statistics and when we talk I sometimes tell her, in the nicest of all possible ways, that she might look to shoot a little more, or that she might want to step out in the passing lane more often on defense, or some such advice that she hardly needs. She has her own coach. But it is that I coached her from the time she was seven until she was fourteen, and it is hard for me to stop being her coach, her father, and if not the former, the latter I will always be.

It is Sunday morning and I help Etsuko wash the dishes from our feast of sourdough waffles, eggs and bacon and coffee with which to build the day. Gunnar and Karla are coming over soon. The women are going to work on the three kimonos while Gunnar and I take Father out to Sauvie Island to hunt ducks. As I load the car with guns and decoys, Bacchus is beside herself with anticipation. Both her father and mother were champion hunting dogs and Bacchus has the gene deep in her blood. There are days when she will sit in the backyard and watch the sky for hours, her neck turning with the flight of ducks and geese. On such days when I come outside without a gun, her disappointment in me is palpable.

With the three women working away amid two languages and great laughter, we drive up Hwy. 26 and then we cut over Germantown Road that takes us down to the Columbia River. It is raining hard and the sky is a gray smear that pushes down upon us. I have Father decked out in a pair of brown waders and a camouflaged rain jacket and hat. We are all dressed essentially the same. Gunnar has already painted his face and now Father is busy applying brown and green to his own. I can sense that he is enjoying all this for he has never hunted duck before, much less fired a gun. As I look in the rearview mirror, I can see him apply the brown paint in thin and careful lines, and then I see that he is writing the kanji for duck on his left cheek. I laugh and tell him the ducks will read his face and fly right into our blind.

"*Chotto matte*," he says. Wait a minute. Gunnar has turned around and watches as Father writes other characters on his right cheek, ones I do not recognize.

"What does that say?" I ask.

He finishes the application and says, "Sukiyaki," and I laugh so hard I almost drive off the winding road into the wild blackberry bushes that comprise a good percentage of Northwestern Oregon. Then I tell Gunnar what it means and he falls into laughter. I look back in the mirror and see Father smile as he reveals a side of his personality that I did not know existed, his face now a menu offering duck sukiyaki. I now know what we are having for dinner.

We cross the bridge over the Multnomah Channel and drive to the other side of the island. The rain is coming down harder now and I hope we can get some ducks early on so that we can go back and have a drink by the fire. This thought marks my age, for in years past it was nothing for me to sit in a wet blind for five or six hours, but now I would rather hunt ducks on a warm, fall day when not a bird flies the sky.

After checking in for a blind, we trudge along a dike that separates the ponds until we find the blind to which we have been assigned. Gunnar wades out into the water and Father and I toss decoys to him. "Hey, not so close," he says when I have splashed him full in the face.

"Sorry," I say and Father laughs. Bacchus is watching Gunnar at work. One winter day, Gunnar and I were hunting geese up on the Columbia River a couple of hours east of Portland. We sat in that blind for a good six hours and we couldn't get any of the geese that flew overhead to come into the cove where we sat watching our decoys. I don't know what it was, my bad calling or maybe they saw us in the blind, but they flew overhead without the least bit of interest in our decoys which bobbed unbothered in the cove. Bacchus had enough of our ineptness, I guess, for she sprinted out of the blind. I yelled for her to stop, but she ignored me and was in the air, and then in the water with a loud splash. Gunnar and I watched as she mouthed a decoy and then swam back with it, ran up the bank with it hanging in from her mouth, dropped it at out feet and then shook herself dry. She looked up at me, her brown eyes pleading for praise, and Gunnar said, "She's right. It's quitting time."

I show Father how to load the gun, how the pump works, how the safety works, and he takes it all in with few questions. He is a quick study. Gunnar has the decoys in a good pattern and he comes out of the water and joins us in the blind. Gunnar can call with the best of them and I let him do most of the work as I whisper instructions to father. "Wait until they drop their feet," I say, "and then start blasting. And keep the butt of the gun tight against your shoulder. Otherwise you'll bruise up pretty good."

Gunnar is calling now and a flock of about thirty teal circle overhead and then they start coming down. I look at father and when I see the kanji on his face I want to laugh, but I stifle my desire. The ducks are talking up a storm now as they come down toward our decoys. I tell father to take his safety off and I do the same. Gunnar is calling so well he has me believing he's a duck. They are coming across the water now, lower and lower, and they cup their wings and drop their feet and we all jump up and start shooting. I knock one down, Gunnar knocks down two and Father has emptied his gun into the air. Bacchus is out of the blind and into the water, and Father says, "I got one."

"Nice shooting," I tell him, not wanting to correct his error. I walk to the water's edge and watch Bacchus retrieve the farthest duck from shore. She swims back toward me, her head held high, a winged duck flopping in her mouth. She brings it up to where I stand and drops it in my hand. It is alive and I have to break its neck. "Go fetch," I tell Bacchus and she is back out in the water. I give her a hand signal to go for the duck to the right and watch as she does so.

"She is a smart dog," Father says. "She is going for the one I shot." Bacchus brings the duck back and then retrieves the third and we go back into the blind. Gunnar takes out a flask of Scotch and I take a sip and shudder with its warmth before passing it to Father who drinks and then wipes his mouth with the back of his hand. We huddle up in the pouring rain, Gunnar working the call, and we bring in three more flocks, getting two mallards first, three the second and four the third when Father really does shoot a duck. It is a cold afternoon and we shiver with the chill. Bacchus, she could stay out in this weather forever as long as there were ducks to retrieve.

"We have plenty for dinner," I say. "Let's get back and see how the kimonos are coming."

On the drive back, Father tells us about the tradition of *Kamo Ryo*, the duck hunts of the Imperial Court. "*Ano ne,*" Father says, "there is a duck reserve at Koshigaya in Saitama Prefecture and another at Niihama in Chiba where they have dug canals near the lake shores. They have planted bamboo next to the canal to hide the hunters who have nets on long poles. They do not use guns. Instead, they scatter feed in the canal and let loose some real live decoy ducks who eat the feed and their feeding calls alert the wild ducks on the lake. They fly into the canal and after they have landed, the hunters frighten the ducks into flight. As they take off, the hunters extend their nets and catch them out of the air."

As I translate this to Gunnar, Gunnar nods his head. This is all new to me, too, so that I am both an eager listener and an interpreter.

"Sometimes," Father says, "a duck escapes and flies off to the lake proper to alert the other ducks. This is when the hawker releases his hawk which pursues and catches the escaping duck."

When I tell this to Gunnar, he asks me to ask Father if he has ever done this.

"No," he says. "This is a sport for the nobility and their guests. But I have made sukiyaki with duck meat." He smiles as he says this. "And if you allow me the honor, I shall cook sukiyaki this evening."

"Of course," I say. "It would be an honor for us."

As we drive back through the darkening rain, I think of getting out of these wet clothes and into the hot tub and then tonight's dinner of steaming sukiyaki and *tokkuri* of hot sake: I am warmed in this contemplation as much as I am by the heater that is blasting at my cold feet.

•

Our apartment was on a small alley at the end of which was situated Tekona, a small shrine built several hundred years before. Early each morning a group of monks walked down our alley to the shrine and I could hear them chanting and beating drums. They were my alarm clock.

Legend has it that Tekona was a young maiden with whom many, many men fell in love. So many of these men declared their love to her that she was disturbed and finally, not wishing to cause misery among these men–for she could not marry them all–she drowned herself. Thus, this shrine was built in her memory and it is believed that women who visit the shrine will have a happily married life. Yamabeno Akahito, a Manyoshu poet, yearned after her thus: "Oh, maid of Teknoa, in thy days of great age, men put on their best belts, built their cottages and came for thy hand. Thy eternal resting place is here, they say; but nought I see save the towering yew trees and a great pine striking out its branches. But thy name, thy story shall never go out of man's memory."

Indeed, there was still a great pine tree that twisted into the sky between the pond and the temple. After returning from Hiroshima by shinkansen, the bullet train, we walked up Daimon Dori through a hard rain, both of us looking forward to a hot bath. Unfortunately, we discovered the hot water heater to be broken. "Let's walk up to the *sento*," I said.

Etsuko agreed and we walked up the alley and cut through the grounds of the shrine as the rain washed off its steeply pitched roof. The public bath was a few blocks beyond the shrine. I had been there only once before, and had always wanted to go again because I liked the salubrious ritual of public bathing.

We paid the woman one-hundred yen each and went our separate ways. Although the *sento* was once co-ed, it was no longer thus. I undressed and placed my clothes in a basket in the changing room before walking through the steamed-over glass doors into a large room the walls and the floor of which were tiled blue. I saw the bath beneath the far wall and I could see three heads in the steam that rose from the large pool. Along the near wall were ten or so spigots about two feet above the floor. Each had an optional shower head at the end of a flexible cord. Before one, a man now sat on an upturned bucket. He was washing his hair.

I took a bucket and sat down and washed myself off from head to toe, and then I rinsed off. The mirror before me was steamed over and I could only vaguely recognize myself. Now that I was clean, I could go bathe.

I stepped into the water and sat down, the water to my neck. Like the others, I placed the small towel on top of my head to keep it from getting wet. When I first came to Japan, I could never have climbed directly into the bath like this for the water is hotter than any spa in the states. It can literally burn you. But once I became used to it, I took a hot bath every night, sometimes soaking in the water for an hour or more. The small tub we had in our apartment could reheat the water as you bathed so you never risked having to get out because of cold water.

There was no talking among the four of us who lounged in the bath, but I could hear the voices of women come over the wall that separated the two bathing areas. I tried to make out Etsuko's voice, but I couldn't discern it from the others who were speaking of things domestic, the price of daikon at the local market, how drunk one woman's husband was when he came home the night before, how one child's kanji had improved after one month of studying after school at a *jyuku*, how one woman had started taking English lessons at one of the numerous English conversation schools near Ichikawa Station. She could have been my student. But I could not hear Etsuko's voice and I wondered: Did the fact that she had married a *gaijin*, blond hair and blue eyes, did that somehow make her less Japanese? Maybe it did, I thought, at least in the eyes of other Japanese. But of course these women would not know that she was married to me. Thus, I surmised as the hot water loosened my joints, massaged my muscles, maybe it was that she felt less who she had been before she married me and she had become slightly more someone else as had I.

I lay back in the bath and imagined my future. I remember imagining my future in that bath. I thought we would move back to Oregon and I would be a successful writer. I thought we would have children. I thought we would be happy. I foresaw a grand future, and I stayed in this hypnotic state for what must have been a long time for when I climbed out of the bath I was surprised at how red my skin had become—the color of a boiled crab. Now I look back at that evening when I was looking forward toward now, and it is thus that the propinquity of time past has spiraled before me.

Etsuko was already in the lobby when I emerged. She asked me how it was, and my answer was a pleasureful sigh. She smiled and took my arm and we walked out into the spring evening. When I turned in the opposite direction of our apartment, she asked me where I wanted to go. "Let's go see if *Kimbe Sushi* is open."

She readily agreed. *Kimbe Sushi* was our favorite sushi restaurant–anywhere. The problem was, you never knew if it would be open. Each day the master would rise at three in the morning and travel to Tsukiji, Tokyo's sprawling fish market. If the fish were not as fresh as he liked, he would simply not open his restaurant that day. After having been to Tsukiji, however, I found it hard to believe that he could not find the fresh fish he desired: the market was literally several square kilometers of thousands of species of fish. But then the master was a perfectionist and that is why we liked to eat there despite the expense. That and he was a connoisseur of sake and he introduced us to many new and profound flavors (I suspected that in truth the reason he sometimes did not open was because of his bibulous nature which might well have caused him to miss some mornings at the fish market).

We were in luck. It was open and there were two seats open at the bar. There were no tables in his restaurant, just the sushi bar that could accommodate a dozen diners. As we sat down, he looked up from his hands which were fast at work slicing a piece of tuna, and he greeted us by name. His wife brought us each an *oshibori* with which we wiped our hands. The heat was soothing, cleansing, and looking at all the clean colors of fish in the glass case that draped the sushi bar somehow seemed spiritually fulfilling. Food is God, I thought, and I worshiped sushi.

I was thirsty from the bath and the first sip of Sapporo was a long one.

"Ah, Etsuko-san," I said. "Life is simply grand."

I clinked her glass and gave the Italian salute, saying, "Chin-chin." In Japanese, this means small penis and thus I always employed the phrase on both solemn and festive occasions. As many good-looking foreigners did, my friend Larry moonlighted as an actor in commercials. He was doing a sake commercial for television where four men were in a public bath drinking sake. Each man was to toast using traditional salutations in French, English, Italian and Spanish. Larry was to say *bottoms up* in English, but when the camera zoomed in on him, he ad-libbed by saying, "*chin-chin*." The Japanese director said cut, and demanded an explanation. Larry explained that it was a real Italian toast, and then he stood up out of the bath, raised his glass to the director and said, "*Chin-chin*." The director looked Larry over and said, "Not so small, but we use your toast."

Estuko and I sat at the counter of *Kimbe Sushi* eating an array of sushi and drinking sake and beer for two hours. My favorite was *amai-ebi* sashimi, sweet shrimp, but not for the shrimp meat itself which was served alive on a plate where it wiggled slightly until I picked it up with my chopsticks and dipped it in the *wasabi* and soy sauce mixture before popping it into my mouth; no, I ordered this for the shrimp's head skeleton which was lightly battered and deep fried. It was a crunchy delight.

●

After we have cleaned the ducks, bathed in the hot tub and showered, we sit in the kitchen drinking hot sake as Father stands at the counter slicing thin strips of duck meat. Outside the rain is beating down in a relentless attack on the night. Bacchus is in the living room lying before the fire, and I wonder if she is remembering her retrieval of the ducks. Can a dog be proud of her accomplishments?

Father recounts the duck hunt to Mother who is sincerely impressed with his having shot a duck. She sits next to me. Across the table are Gunnar and Karla. Etsuko is busying herself at the counter making *sunomono*, a salad of pickled cabbage. "Father is a good shot," I tell her and she laughs and says, "But he has never shot a gun."

"I know, but he is a quick learner. After three flocks of ducks came over our blind, the word was out among the survivors. No more ducks would fly near us, so we came home."

Mother smiles and says, "*Honto*?"

"Yes, really. Ducks are smart. They didn't see any humor in

reading *sukiyaki* on Father's face."

Father laughs, turns to us from the counter and says, "He's teasing you, Mother. Don't you know?"

Mother blushes and Etsuko tells me to be nice.

Father has finished slicing the duck. He has already sliced scallions, tofu, bamboo shoots, shitaki mushrooms, and bean sprouts, and he has made a sauce of *mirin*, sugar, soy sauce and water.

Etsuko brings the bowls of *sunomono*, and as father prepares our dinner, we sit at the table drinking hot sake, and nibbling the pickled cabbage until father is ready to present us with his repast.

"When is Elin coming home?" Karla asks.

"Thursday."

Gunnar takes the *tokkuri* of sake and fills all of our glasses. I refill the *tokkuri* and take it to the stove where I set it in a pan of simmering water.

"How long will she stay?"

"Just a couple of days. They're playing Oregon and Oregon State. She'll be here Friday between games. We're going to Eugene for the Duck game," I say.

"Do you have extra tickets?" Gunnar asks.

"Gunnar, we can't go. You have that reception on Saturday."

"Oh, right I forgot." Gunnar looks miffed and I know why. He is a humble and shy man and does not like public attention. Saturday night, the Oregon Book Society is holding a reception in his honor. As his friend, I should go, of course, but I know he sincerely does not care if I do; in fact, he would rather I not as he would feel all the more embarrassed if I were in attendance to witness his being honored. He had told me as much: "Take your in-laws to Eugene to see the game, for Christ's sake," he said. "In fact, get me a ticket and I'll go too. They can honor me in absentia. Most of it is just so they can hear themselves make speeches, anyway."

I can hear the suet sizzle in the pan, and I watch as father carefully lays slices of duck on the hot surface. He adds all the vegetables in the corner of the huge cast iron sukiyaki pan, but not the scallions. Her pours in the sauce, and I can smell the duck now, and I know that Bacchus must be jealous in the living room for she can smell a meal a mile away. Or maybe she is lying there proud to have been part provider?

Father cooks for five more minutes, turning the meat and vegetables with the long cooking chopsticks, and he adds the scallions. Finally the meal is ready and he carries the skillet to the table where he sets it on the wooden Lazy Susan at the center of the table.

Etsuko and I serve the rice and the bowls with raw egg in which we dip the meat, and we are ready to dine.

"Tell Father it smells wonderful," Karla says.

Etsuko translates and Father says, "I hope you will like it. I have not made sukiyaki in a long time and never with my own duck." I can see the pride in his posture as he says this and I am satisfied sitting in a kitchen drinking hot sake with people I hold so dear and I think of the Tao: *Knowing others is wisdom;/Knowing the self is enlightenment./Mastering others requires force;/Mastering the self needs strength./He who knows he has enough is rich./Perseverance is a sign of will power./He who stays where he is endures. To die but not to perish is to be eternally present.*

●

I am up early again and Bacchus and I walk the trail to the pond. Cindy, my editor, called at 6 a.m. this morning as I was making coffee. I answered the phone both quickly and gruffly. She had forgotten the time difference, she said, but I know she did not; it was just a convenient time for her to call, it being 9 a.m. in New York. She told me that she doubted she could publish my memoir, and when I asked her why, she said that it lacked a firm direction. I told her that looking back was more tumescent than looking forward and that the next time she called she ought to have the manners to wait until her sun has moved a bit farther west. I know that to be fatuous, but then why pretend we understand the nature of time? I hung up the phone and now I find myself walking through the fog with a dog who knows no frustration, who has no ill will, and I wish I were more of a dog and less of a man. When I think of pit bulls bred to fight, my ire rises so that I want to kill the men who raise them. Show me a mean dog, and you've revealed a malevolent man.

Publishing is an affair of whimsy, and thus many good manuscripts are left without covers while a great amount of sensational crap is bound but unfortunately not gagged. I have had my own share of frustrations over the years, and I wonder why we bother to write; but then I know it is not so much a choice as a need, and the fact that much of our fine work remains unpublished is simply another example of how money can corrupt art. An earlier novel of mine was liked by an editor at HarperCollins, but at an acquisitions meeting the Trade Paperback people said it would not sell enough in paperback, so the novel was left unacquired. Be sure to note that to be *left unacquired* is as bleak as it sounds.

Sometimes as I sit here at this desk, I wonder, ah, the hell with it, I will go on and write this despite what Cindy thinks.

•

"When shall we go to America?" Etsuko asked as we sat drinking green tea at the *kotatsu* in our apartment in Ichikawa. It was a clear day in March, clear but cold and the kerosene heater burned in the living room where we sat, a tea kettle of water steaming atop the stove to take some of the aridity out of the air.

"That's a bit out of the blue," I said. "More tea?" I held the pot above her cup, but she shook her head. I refilled my own cup.

"Out of the blue?"

"A bit of a non sequitur."

"And what is that?"

"Something that does not logically follow that which proceeds it."

113

"What are you talking about? That, then, is out of the blue."

"Not so, my little harbor seal. Out of the blue means that something just came to you seemingly from nowhere. For example: I would like to lick your breasts with my tongue."

"How else could you lick them? You are redundant."

"True. But also out of the blue."

I stretched my leg out under the *kotatsu* and nudged her feet. Then I heard a voice blaring through a loudspeaker breaking the afternoon silence, the voice carried on a truck all the while getting closer. I understood some of what the man was saying, mostly *vote for Kando Ichiro* over and over again.

Etsuko said, "It is time for the erection again," to which I responded, "yes, indeed."

"Jake, you know what I mean."

"Yes, yes. I know what you mean. The battle of L's and R's."

"So, when do we go to America?"

"You make it sound like a song. When would you like to go?"

"Soon. Jake?"

She looked like she was going to cry. "What is it?"

"I think I am pregnant."

I smiled and crawled around the *kotatsu* on my hands and knees and took her in my arms and we lay back on the *tatami* and I hugged and kissed her, hugged them both.

"Why are you crying?" I asked.

"Because I am happy. You're not mad?"

"How could I be mad? The woman I love most in the world is having my baby. This is the happiest day in my life since you said you would marry me. I am thrilled."

We sat up and she said, "Jake? What I said? Is that something that would be considered out of the blue?"

"Oh, Etsuko, there has never been anything said that is so that."

"Then when do you think we will go?"

"Go?"

"To America?"

"When would you like?"

"Soon. Next month."

"Okay, my sweet dear, next month it is. We will move to the states, to America as you say, next month, and we will have our little sweet baby born there, and we will be happy as clams, and..."

"Happy as clams? Why clams?"

"At high tide." And I went on to explain the colloquialism as I did explain all the strange idioms I used, and I thought, yes, happy as clams at high tide where no one can bother our bliss.

As we lay in the angled light of afternoon, I thought about our future. I wondered what I would do once back in the states, would I teach, would I have the time to write, would I make enough money to support a family, a wife and a child? I have never been a worrier, but I was now pinned down with anxiety. I knew, however, the worry would go away once I had some plan.

So it was. The next month, at the end of the school year, I quit my job and we took a train to Kobe, Japan, from whence we took a boat to Shanghai, China, and we spent a month traveling in China before flying from Hong Kong to, as Etsuko put it, America, a country where we would live and raise a beautiful girl named Elin who would be the joy of both of our worlds.

•

As I drive up the interstate through a dark night washed with a constant wall of rain, I listen to Elin talk to her grandparents who sit in the back seat on either side of her. The dashboard lights set Etsuko's face aglow, and it is a sweet smile of nostalgia I can see she wears. Maybe she is recalling her own childhood with these two people surrounding her with love as they now do with her own daughter, with mine. I feel the warmth of love and I reach and take Etsuko's hand in mine. She looks at me and we lock eyes and her smile grows.

115

Father is telling Elin how impressed he is with her game. She came up with a steal with thirty seconds left to seal a three point win, and as Father tells her about each shot she made, I blush with pride and am glad the car is dark. Mother tells her much the same.

Elin's Japanese is fluent and her accent is Japanese. Her only flaw is her occasional lapse in vocabulary, but that is something that would be repaired after only a few months in Japan where she plans to spend this coming summer. Now, in the back seat of my car, she is being absolutely bathed with love by two people who rarely see her and I know how sad they must feel when they are so far away in Japan and they think of their only granddaughter. The longing they must feel surely must rent their breasts.

Dinner is a week away, and I find I am nervous. Nervous and righteous, too, I suppose. I am of torn desire: at once, I would like to rip their throats out, and yet I would like to convert them to good human beings. What does this admixture of desire say about me, me whom I consider to be a good human being? Hard to say. As I drive, I remember this from the Tao: *Heaven and Earth are ruthless;/ They see the ten thousand things as dummies./The wise are ruthless;/They see the people as dummies./The space between heaven and earth is like a bellows./ The shape changes but not the form;/The more it moves, the more it yields./ More words count less./Hold fast to the center.* And now I am in the fast lane.

While I was working on the memoir this morning, stuck in trying to find a point of embarkation from which to move Etsuko and me from Shanghai to the states, the phone rang. It was the bailiff, Milton Miles, who is to attend our dinner on Friday. He just wanted to "firm things up" and he went on to say that these three punks were incorrigible and that no amount of raw fish would render them human, something I thought funny in my understanding of the word *render* and one of its tertiary meanings: to melt down and remove the impurities

116

from. And that's what we will try to do. We will render the hell out of all three.

Now I take Bacchus out back to the herb garden where I spade the soil. Though it is winter, I enjoy digging in the dirt in that somehow touching the earth, growing food, brings me closer to our shared soul and it is in the dirt and from the dirt where we are and were one. Sometimes I will grab a handful of soil and sprinkle it from my fingers, and there are times when I walk through fields of black, loamy soil when I would like to burrow in it head first to find the secrets of time.

Bacchus struts around the yard with her head held up high, her nose fast at work, maybe to discern any interlopers who might be within range, someone who could bestow upon her a nice pat, a belly rub, a tickle of the ears. She spies a squirrel digging for buried treasure, and she runs after it, barking madly. The squirrel literally high tails it, runs up the base of a Fuji apple tree, and stops on the first branch six feet above where Bacchus now runs in circles, barking like some feral beast placed in the wrong century and wanting to get out. The squirrel is composed in the knowledge that dogs can't climb trees and it calmly peers down at Bacchus. If the squirrel had something to throw, that is what it would do. "Bacchus," I yell. "Enough." She pays me no heed, and continues in her crazed state until I walk over to her with a tennis ball and throw it across the yard into the sedge where she chases it, her memory of the squirrel released like a caged bird sent free.

As I turn the soil, this the top of the earth, its very crust, I think that I am now content here in this garden of ours, happy with no desire to move, and again I think of the Tao: *Knowing others is wisdom; Do you think you can take over the universe and improve it?/I do not believe it can be done./The universe is sacred./You cannot improve it./If you try to change it, you will ruin it./If you try to hold it, you will lose it./So sometimes things are ahead and sometimes they are behind;/Sometimes breathing is hard, sometimes it comes easily;/Sometimes there is strength and sometimes weakness; Sometimes one is up and sometimes down./Therefore the sage avoids extremes, excesses, and complacency.*

So much wisdom in so few words.

Bacchus is back with the ball. She drops it at my feet. Her tail cannot possibly move any faster, and she stares down at the ball first cocking her head so as to view the ball with her right eye, then cocking her head the other way as if to verify what she has seen with her left eye. "Bacchus," I say. "Let's go live up to your name sake." I head toward the garage, and Bacchus picks up the ball and trots beside me.

I pour an amber ale into her dish, then open one for myself. As she laps up the ale, I sit down on the doorstep and sip my own. Etsuko comes out into the garage and says, "Ah ha. Just as I thought. You and your dog drinking beer."

"It was her idea. I didn't want her to drink alone. Join us?"

"Not right now. We're busy planning the menu."

"Ah," I say. "The menu."

She goes back inside, and her mentioning the menu has served as the catalyst for another beer. As I pop the top, Bacchus lies down and eyes me. "Another beer, Bacchus?" I ask.

She stands and wags her tail. What the hell, I think: it's better not to drink alone. I pour the contents of the bottle into her dish, go to the refrigerator and grab another. I sit back down on the step and drink. Bacchus laps hers up greedily, as if she feels I may push her aside and lap it up myself. She has her backside to me, her tail straight down between her legs. When she finishes, she looks up, stretches, and yawns. She comes and lies on the rug at my feet so that I can rub her belly. "You're a sot today, Bacchus, and me, I am an enabler." I rub her belly with my foot as I slowly sip my ale and ponder the events on the horizon. I have always thought I could change the way people think, more so when I was younger, of course, but still I continue to think I can exact change no matter how small the coinage. If I did not think I could, what would be the point in writing, in living? It seems we should all want to make the world better without wanting only for ourselves. I understand there are those who do not feel this way. I know there are those who wish only for themselves, and they have even rationalized and deceived themselves into believing that their own hard work and their resulting piles of gold actually help the rest of the world. They worship the 18th century philosopher Adam Smith, and though they are always reaching for more, they cannot see their hands in the pot.

But me: I believe I can educate. In the classroom, I have always believed I could make the students more humanist, more caring, less biased, less prejudiced, more understanding as well for in teaching literature the first thing one must teach is empathy for if the student cannot learn to empathize, he cannot digest literature. Once he has learned to empathize, and then when he has learned to truly understand character-driven literature, he will finally be prepared to be an empathetic human being stripped bare of his pre-disposed prejudice.

Some years back, I had twin sisters in a composition class. The assignment was to write a definition essay. One of the twins wrote a brilliant essay about what it meant to be a lesbian. She wrote about all the secret pain she had suffered growing up as she heard her friends make disparaging remarks about gays and lesbians. This went on for years until she finally "came out" as they say.

Our class was comprised of the usual mixture of students, and in the back row were several jocks one of whom weeks earlier had made a disparaging comment about gays. I told him I would not allow such language in my classroom, and he smirked and went quiet. The day I was returning the definition essays to the students, I asked the young woman if she would read her essay to the class. She acquiesced to my invitation, albeit reluctantly, and the class was quiet as she stood before them reading what it meant to be a lesbian, a person so often vilified by others.

Still, to this day, tears well up in my eyes when I remember her standing there before us, tears on her own cheeks as she read about how she was still the victim of the hatred of others. Those boys in the back of the class, I watched them as she read, I watched all the students, and there was not one who was unaffected by what she wrote. No matter how much or how little, her reading her essay before them changed them all for the rest of their lives. When she was done reading, everyone clapped, even the boys in the back, and I was not the only one who cried.

One thing I have never been able to understand is how people can harbor senseless hate, and these people who hate men and women of a different color and of a different sexual orientation are more often than not Christians who smack bibles against their thighs causing a knee-jerk reaction to all they do not understand. Unfortunately, when one has been blinded by religion, there is little to do in trying to get him to see the light.

Bacchus breaks my reverie with her snoring at one end, and her farting at the other. This reminds me of when Elin was small. One of her daily chores was to feed and water Bacchus. One day, I asked her to go out in the yard and clean up Bacchus' scat, and she quipped, "Dad, I've got the front end. It's you who's got the back end."

I leave Bacchus to her nap and go inside to check on the menu. There is one dish I would like to include.

Raw *fugu* served whole.

Last night, I found myself reading in bed when Etsuko came in and joined me. The expression *I found myself* is really not as odd as it sounds, either, if one stops to think how our subconscious and conscious separate themselves and only on occasion do we allow ourselves to wholly slip into the subconscious and when this happens, of course, it is our conscious who has found ourselves enjoying the moment away. Thus, I now understand what my sixth grade teacher meant when he told the class he had been to Seattle over the weekend and that he drove the 180 miles back asleep. Of course, I told my father that, and I remember him saying, "Bullshit. What kind of teachers do you have today? Probably all on acid." But now I know what my teacher meant: he had slipped into the subconscious on the drive home.

I am reading Cormac McCarthy's *All the Pretty Horses*. I have read everything he has written at least once, and several of his novels twice. He is one of the best writers we have today not only because of the stories he tells, but because of the way he utilizes language, composing sentences so inherently beautiful as to make other writers foolish with jealousy.

Etsuko crawls beneath the sheets and pulls the blanket up to her neck. I set my book down and turn off the light. "I'm so tired," she says.

I lean over and kiss her on the cheek. "Get a good night's sleep, and you'll be better in the morning."

"Jake?"

"What is it?"

"Do you think I am doing the right thing?"

"You mean the dinner?"

"Yes. The dinner. Having three racist skinheads over for dinner."

I think about this. "Etsuko, you have the right motive, and that, I believe, is enough. Whether you can change their thinking, I don't know. But you are right about one thing: Prison would only make them worse. Especially the youngest one. What was his name?"

"Keegan. Keegan Porter. The smallest one with the red hair."

I lean on my elbow and stroke her hair. "He seems the most gullible. Malleable like clay. A week with him, and I could convince him of the importance of literature, and he would sincerely believe."

"That other one, he scares me."

"The big one? The oaf?"

"No, not him. The one who never smiled. Not once. Daniel Dunn."

"Yes. He's probably already completely brainwashed. He's the one we'll offer tainted sushi."

"Not funny."

"I know. I just don't know how to reach him, how we could possibly get him to see how wrong he is. He's an intelligent young man, but something's happened to him. Did you see his eyes?" I lie back and sigh.

"Yes. He could stare through a wall. In prison, he would find a lot of young men like Keegan and he'd create an army. He scares me."

"When you were in school, did you read John Steinbeck's *Of Mice and Men*?"

"In high school. We read it in English, too, and I remember how difficult that was."

"Then you remember Lenny. The other guy, Leonard Harmon, he reminds me of Lenny. He has that goofy smile. He even has the name."

"Yes, he seems a bit slow."

"Well, Etsuko, my little diplomat, maybe the dinner is a good idea. I know we're not going to change them a lot, maybe only a little, but I agree with you that this is better than prison. It's just that another part of me would like to break a beer bottle over their heads."

Etsuko rolls over on top of me and kisses me. "Jake, another part of me would, too, but then we would start a war."

I hug her and she hugs me, and I wonder if those three young men had anyone to hug or be hugged by, especially today when everyone is afraid of being charged with molestation. What kind of country is this when you cannot hug someone without being afraid of being arrested? A child cries and you cannot touch her when human touch is exactly what she needs.

In the morning, there is a light frost leaving our world whitened. I let Bacchus out the back door and watch her as she slips on the patio before trotting off into the yard, her nose taking everything in. I make a pot of coffee and then I start to fry a pan of bacon before taking the sourdough batter out of the oven where I have left it overnight with the door ajar, the oven light keeping it at the right temperature. Last night, I added two cups of flour and two cups of water to the starter, and now I take off a few spoonfuls and place it in a jar and put it in the refrigerator for next week. I add two eggs, two tablespoons of sugar, one teaspoon of salt and three table spoons of melted bacon grease to the bowl of batter. When it is time to cook, I will add a half teaspoon of baking soda, and when I whip it into the frothy batter, it will magically rise.

Etsuko joins me at the kitchen counter, and I pour her a mug of coffee. Bacchus comes to the back door with the newspaper in her mouth, and I take a piece of bacon from the pan, blow on it and wipe off the oil with a paper towel. I open the door, and Bacchus drops the paper at my feet. "Good dog, Bacchus," I tell her and I give her the piece of bacon which she eats with pleasure. I wipe her feet and she trots into the kitchen and goes to her mat by the garage door where she lies down.

"Waffles or pancakes this morning?" I ask.

"Blueberry pancakes, please." Etsuko turns a page of the paper. "There's an article about Gunnar's book in the books section."

"Really?" I remove the bacon from the pan and place it in the oven. "What does it say?"

"Well, you wrote it, so I guess you'd probably know."

"Ah, that's right. I did write it. Do you think he'll be pleased?"

"Of course, Jake. It's very laudatory."

"Well, it was a good book."

Father and Mother join Etsuko at the counter, and I fry up pancakes and eggs. This is our Sunday morning ritual, the sourdough breakfast, a ritual my father always conducted for our family when I was young, and now I carry it on into the future so although my father is dead, he will never really die. He will live on in my actions and gestures as will I through Elin's, and in that, we are immortal and connected to this earth.

"Are you going to make a kimono for the bailiff as well?" I ask Etsuko.

"I hadn't thought of that. I suppose we should."

Her mother agrees. They will need more silk, she says, and she asks if we can take her to the store.

"It'll take a lot of silk, for he's a big man," Etsuko says. "Jake, what's his name?"

"Milton. Milton Miles. Anyone for more pancakes?"

Everyone has eaten enough, it seems, and I suggest a walk to father who readily agrees. We bundle up and head out the door with

Bacchus, mother and daughter sitting at the counter together, drinking coffee, talking and laughing, a pretty sight to behold.

We walk along the gravel drive to the main road, the sky hanging low with dark clouds, and I notice what appears to be a for sale sign on my property, though from the back I cannot really tell. When we get to the end of the drive, I see what the sign says: *Race Mixers Will Burn in Hell.* I feel the rage swell up in my chest, the blood gone wild, the heat up my back and neck so that I am perspiring despite the morning's chill. Father asks me what it is, and I tell him and he shakes his head. I pull up the sign and we turn and walk back toward the house, Bacchus the only one of us still cheerful and oblivious of some man's incongruous hate now turned crime.

An hour later, the police have arrived, two young county cops, a man and a woman. In the kitchen, they conduct their inquiry.

"Any idea who did this?" The man asks. The woman, she is posed with pen in hand ready to write down what I say.

I explain about the three skinheads and our upcoming dinner. The male cop sneers and says, "They should be in jail. That's what we do with bad guys in this country. We put them in jail"

"I doubt it was them," Etsuko says.

"Then who?" The female cop asks.

"Who knows?" I say. "It could be anyone. Go file your report. It won't do any good, but do file it."

"Does this sort of thing happen a lot?" The woman asks.

"No," I say.

"Well, then, it's probably just an isolated incident. I wouldn't worry about it."

"What?" I shout. "We shouldn't worry about it when someone anonymously posts a sign in our yard, on our property, a sign condemning our marriage. You wouldn't fucking worry about it?"

"Easy," the male cop says. "She didn't mean anything."

"Right. She didn't mean anything."

"Jake," Etsuko says. Mother and Father watch with concern.

"I'm sorry," the woman says. "I just meant that I don't think that this is a physical threat."

"No?" I say. "Not a threat? Then what?"

"Well..."

"You can leave now. I don't think you'll be any help to us."

"Call us if anything else transpires," the man says. "We'll be in touch if we learn anything."

"Right," I say. "See if she learns anything."

I close the door behind them and my first thought is of my guns.

I have kept my three shotguns in a locked gun cabinet in my office for many years, but now I put one under the bed, one in the front hall closet, and one in the closet in the pantry off the kitchen, hiding shells near each one. If some son of a bitch comes calling with malicious intent, I intend to be prepared. That is what I tell Etsuko. She knows how to use the guns, the pump, the semi-automatic and the double-barrel, but she is not pleased with their new location and tells me so that night after Mother and Father have gone to bed. "Jake," she says. "You are over-reacting."

"I am simply being prepared. If I need a gun quick, I'll have one at hand."

"You are not going to need a gun." She sets down her cup of chamomile tea. Me, I am sipping a short glass of Maker's Mark, neat.

"I hope you're right, but in the event you are wrong, I'll be ready."

"What are you going to do? Shoot someone?"

"If I have to."

"You really would?"

"Damn right I really would. Those are all twelve gauges. I'd kill the sons of bitches if they came with the intent to harm us. That is what we call self-defense."

"Jake, I have never seen you like this. With so much hate. You're not a violent man."

"I am becoming one. I just might have to be violent."

125

She stands and comes behind me and wraps her arms around my shoulders, around my neck, and she kisses the top of my head. "Jake, honey, I love you. Calm yourself." She stands there holding me, and I feel the violence melt until warm tears trickle down my cheeks. I turn and take her in my arms and we hold each other for a short forever.

•

It is morning, and I am at my desk writing this which I consider to be a memoir although a good part of it is in the present and is yet to be digested as memory. This brings to mind the fact that we are all traveling into the future together in the same time machine, though when most people think of a time machine they want one to travel at much greater speeds which is silly, of course, in that what would their intended destination be? Anywhen but now, I suppose. If we consider time to be comprised of the past, the present and the future as our verb tenses reflect, it is strange that most people do not live at all for in the present they are anticipating and preparing for the future, and when they arrive they find themselves still looking beyond where they now stand so that they are like a fast moving train that roars through each station where, if the train would only stop, they would find what we call life, but their train is in perpetual advance and they hang on looking ahead at what they consider to be their progress, which, if one is to consider the nature of the circle, might just as well be called regress.

Etsuko is off to the store with Mother and Father as there are only three days left before THE DINNER as I refer to it now in all caps. The police called this morning to report that there has been no progress in detecting who left the sign at the foot of my drive. I don't expect them to find out who did it until whoever it is does it again, that or something similar. I imagine their hate to feel fallow until they manifest it whole by parading it before their victims, and I do not like the idea of being a victim. That is why the shotguns have been so strategically placed, each ready to fire.

126

I hear Bacchus bark from the living room which usually means someone is driving up the gravel drive. It is probably Gunnar as he is coming out this morning to help me organize our final selections of an anthology we have been asked to edit. The anthology consists of work done by writers and poets the university has had visit this past decade. Gunnar wanted me involved because of my work in bringing various writers to campus, but the university was very reluctant to bring me back into their realm because of the beer-tossing incident, but Gunnar convinced them that we would work at home and thus, I would be in no proximity of any of their fine students or faculty.

I meet Gunnar at the door and suggest a walk before we get to work. Though it is cold, now slightly above freezing, pogonip encasing the grass so that it crunches beneath our feet, there is not a cloud in the sky on this February morning, and the sun and blue sky make me feel very, very good. We walk slowly down the path toward the pond, Bacchus up ahead in a steady trot, nose working hard. Every once in a while she turns to see that we are coming, for she enjoys company, and in seeing us she turns and continues on.

"Want to hear a new poem I'm working on?" Gunnar asks. We walk side by side and he doesn't even turn to look at me. I know him to be shy about his work despite how good it is. It is as though he is embarrassed to have such talent, maybe thinking that it should be shared and not wholly his. He is generous in that way.

"Of course. I'm all ears."

"I call it "Tides." It goes like this." We walk more slowly now, and I see that Gunnar has his eyes closed. "I have no desire/to fish empty rivers/to till fallow soil/to drink desert sand./Nor do I wish for/pockets full of money/to buy back the moon/to stall the tides:/I like the slap/of water on my shore,/its lazy retreat/its return, its bearing of gifts/long lost in the depths/a sudden rise of quail." He stops and opens his eyes. He turns to me and smiles. "What do you think?"

"I like it, Gunnar. I really do. I like the sense of our need for surprise, for hope."

"Yes." We continue walking down the path. The air is cold on my face, but the sun is rising higher. There is warmth here walking with my friend.

"We should be out fishing on a morning like this. The steelhead are in the Wilson."

"I love that river."

"I do, too. You want to scuttle our plans for work this morning?"

"I didn't bring any gear."

We have arrived at the pond to find Bacchus chasing a nutria into the water. It disappears and Bacchus is left barking at the water's edge, her tail wagging fiercely. "I have plenty. We could be down there in an hour. Fish for two. Hell, we'd be back here by two o'clock."

"That's what we always say. But we never are. We'll be late."

I give Gunnar a playful punch on the shoulder. "I know. But at least we always go with good intentions of coming back to work. I'll tell you what. We'll bring the stories and poems with us, and we can discuss them as I drive. What do you say?"

"It is a beautiful morning."

"And the river is not empty."

"And we won't be drinking desert sand."

We laugh, call Bacchus and head back to the house.

Bacchus wanted to come in the worst way, but I can't have her in the driftboat when we're fishing because she gets too excited and makes too much noise in the aluminum boat. I've left her outside today as she will enjoy the weather. She has been trained not to leave the property, so I have no worries for her, and Etsuko and her parents will take her in if the weather turns.

Now, Gunnar sits in the stern and I sit in the middle oaring us around a bend in the river, the title of a fine novel by V.S. Naipaul. We are deep in a canyon and though the sun hits the west bank where the alder trees are thick beneath the Douglas firs, we are in the shadows. I drop anchor just above a gentle tailout and we let the current work our lines. I have a Thermos with hot coffee spiked with Maker's Mark

Whisky, and it warms my chest. A blue heron wades in the shallows, its neck bent, alert, stepping gingerly, one knee bending, then the other, as it peers through the water for small fry. Above us, two red tailed hawks drift on the thermals, and I think of my father. Whenever we saw a hawk when I was a boy, he would always say to me, "There's our friend the hawk," and I never asked him why he said that. I just took it for granted that he was right: the hawk *was* our friend. But now, a year after his death, I would like to ask him why he said that. What was the secret meaning behind those words? I think my father would have liked to be a poet, but he grew up during the depression in Golden Valley, North Dakota, and poems did not fill the bread basket–not that they do now.

"Pass the Thermos," Gunnar says, breaking me from my reverie.

I hand it to him, watch him twist it open, the steam rising as he fills his cup. Just then his rod tip slams down. He sets the cup down on the seat beside him, pulls the rod from the pole holder anchored to the gunwale, and he stands and pulls the tip of the rod up into the air. I reel in and reach for the Thermos, close it, and sit back and watch.

The fish is taking out line, and Gunnar, with rod tip high in the air, allows it to make its run. I watch the line as it moves through the water, first to the east bank, and then up river, behind me, past the bow, so that Gunnar has to turn. He dips the rod tip down as he reels quickly, and then pulls the rod tip back up again, and as he does this, the silver steelhead explodes from the water, then slaps back down, and it runs toward the boat as Gunnar reels madly to keep the line from going slack. "Shit, Gunnar. I thought you were going to play him out," I say as I stand to get the net ready. "What's your damn hurry?"

"It's the fish, not me."

"Would you like some of your coffee before it gets cold?"

"Not likely."

The fish takes another run, this time downstream toward the tailout where, if it succeeds in getting there, it could break the line in the shallow rapids on one of the many rocks that jut just beneath the surface. "Keep him from getting down there," I needlessly tell Gunnar as he reels down and then up, and then down, the rod tip moving toward the port side of the boat in his effort to keep the fish from heading back toward the ocean which is only about seven or eight miles away.

He has the fish up above the rapids now, and it is making a run back upriver. This fish is bright, just out of the ocean, well fed on plankton and herring, and it is as powerful as a lumberjack's arm. Again, it breaks the water's surface, almost dancing on its tail before crashing back below, spray sparkling in the sunlight. The sun has risen high enough now where we are bathed in its golden warmth, and *I feel good* standing here with my legs straddling the middle bench of my driftboat with my very good friend fighting a twelve or thirteen pound steelhead in the icy water of the Wilson River on a late morning in February when the rest of the world is, at least during this moment, as inconsequential to us as time itself.

Gunnar is bringing the fish toward the boat now. It is slapping at the water, in and out, above and below, and I ready the net, my right hand on the handle, my left pulling back the loose netting so that I can scoop it out of the water, and as I thrust, the fish dives down, the line zzzzzing off the reel, the water splashing my face off the line.

"That's a hell of a fish," I say.

Gunnar reels, then brings the rod tip up, then reels down, and the fish is again being brought close to the boat, and this time I dip down, net him, kneel down, hold the fish in the water with my hands, and verify that it does not have an adipose fin for we are allowed only to keep fin-clipped hatchery fish. "It's a keeper, Gunnar. And it's a hen, thirteen, fourteen pounds. Maybe fifteen. It'll be full of eggs."

Gunnar sits down, smiles, pours himself some coffee as I unhook the fish and put it in the fish box. "That was fun, Jake. Jesus, what a rush."

"It is a beautiful fish. I thought you'd lose him when he ripped down toward the tailout."

"Me too. He was so strong."

"He jumped about three feet above the water like a damn

torpedo."

"My heart's still pounding. Look, my hands are shaking. See?" He holds his cup of coffee up and I can see it throb.

"Yep."

I pour myself more coffee. The sweet scent of bourbon wafts above my mug. It is sweet and warms me from the inside as now the sun does from the outside on this cold winter morning. An osprey glides above us, continues down river with one flap of its wings as it fishes from the high-above.

I cast out and let the current take my chartreuse yarn down the river, feeling the lead bounce along the river bottom. Gunnar sits and looks out at the river, a secret smile on his face, one that I know not to interrupt. He is now in a state of bliss, and should be left alone. I oblige, retract my line, cast again and let the river do the work until I need to reel in again, the warm hand of the sun on my back, two friends on a river, fishing, having caught something sublime.

On the drive home, we stop at the tavern in Hoquam. It is like entering a dark cave, but there is a fire in the fireplace, and two octogenarians sit at the bar sipping glasses of thin lager, each wearing jeans and plaid shirts, heavy workboots hefted on the rails of their stools. They both have caps on; one has a picture of a cow above which it says Tillamook Cheese, and the other says Massey Ferguson Tractors. The bartender is a withered woman, possibly jaded from years at this isolated outpost where retired loggers drink away lonely afternoons, thinking back to winter days of setting chokers on steep, muddy hillsides in the fecund miasma of this deep winter forest that abounds.

Above the mirror behind the bar is the bust of a six-point bull elk. The walls are adorned with the heads of animals long since dead, deer and elk and sundry fowl, and on a platform in the corner, there is the entire body of a cougar posed to pounce, and I notice now as we sit down at the bar that its eyes have been fitted with one green and one red light bulb and they blink intermittently giving it an eerie effect so that if, indeed, it were able to pounce it would hug you and sing Merry

Christmas. Through the mirror, I notice that there is a bear behind the door we came through, a bear standing on his hind legs, its forelegs stretched high, its visage stretched in a cruel growl.

"What are you two boys drinking?" She comes before us, tosses a coaster in front of each of us, and as she speaks, I see she has no teeth. I wonder if maybe the cougar somehow pulled them out.

"A couple of IPA's," I say.

"We don't have any of that fancy-pantsy IPA here," she says. "Budweiser on tap. Or we have canned beers. Olympia. Blitz. Hamms. Miller."

"Gunnar?"

"Give us a pitcher of Bud, please," he says.

As she fill the pitcher, she asks what we have been up to on this fine February day.

I tell her we've been fishing, and then Tillamook asks if we caught anything.

"Gunnar here caught a nice, bright fifteen pound hen."

"Yeah? Well, good for you," he says. Then he takes a sip of beer, a real small sip like he's trying to make that one glass last all day long. It couldn't have been big enough to swallow, and it was hardly even wet.

Massey says, "You gonna put up the roe? 'Cause if you ain't, I'll buy it off you."

"We eat it."

At the same time, they both say, "You what?"

"Eat it."

The bartender sets two glasses before us, and the pitcher in between. As I pour, I tell them how in Japan salmon eggs, when cured properly, are a delicacy used in sushi and that the eggs of steelhead are equally delightful. "And when they're fresh like these, they just pop in your mouth."

"I'll be god damned," Tillamook says. "I'll be flat god damned. Those Japanese will eat just about anything, I reckon." He has a wad of chewing tobacco in his cheek, and he leans over a Folgers coffee can now

132

and spits. "I'll be plain god damned."

"I heard they eat raw fish," Massey says.

"Sashimi," I tell them. "And sushi is when it is on rice. You guys never ate anything raw before?"

"Hell no," says Tillamook. "Well, an oyster, I guess. Down at Yaquina Bay. The boys bought a bushel of them and we got so drunk we couldn't get a fire going. So we ate them raw. And I'll tell you something. They weren't half bad."

"I wouldn't eat an oyster like that. No way in hell," Massey says.

I take a long sip of Budweiser. "Well, if I can drink this, you guys can try raw fish." I turn to the bartender. "Do you have any soy sauce? A jar of Beaver Foods horseradish, maybe?"

"I believe we do, yessir, I believe we may just have some." She goes to the kitchen, and I take another sip of beer and tell Gunnar I'll be right back. I head out to the rig, and I take my Buck knife from the sheath and open the cooler where that big, silver steelhead glistens on a bed of ice. I cut a good size piece of the cheek, and I head back into the tavern where I see the bartender has a plate set out next to a jar of horseradish and a bottle of Kikoman soy sauce. "I'll need a bowl," I tell her, and when she brings one, I pour in a half inch of soy sauce and then mix in two teaspoons of the horseradish. On the plate, I cut the fish into bite size pieces.

"You don't have chopsticks, do you?"

"Does this look like a Chinese restaurant to you? You gonna want a fortune cookie, too?"

"How about some forks?"

"Forks I can do."

She scurries off into the kitchen again, and comes back with five forks. "It would taste better with chopsticks, but these forks will have to do. Now, Gunnar, I have never had sashimi steelhead before, but I have had everything else, so I am sure this will be very good. It's only an hour out of the water and it's been on ice, gentlemen. I propose a toast. You'll need a glass," I tell the bartender.

"You buying me a beer?"

"Sure."

"Okay." She draws a glassful from the tap. She slurps off the foam with lips bent inward so that not being dentigerous seems almost natural and well suited, for drinking at least.

I stand and raise my glass. Gunnar smiles. "Let us toast to the fish we are about to eat, and to the fine gentlemen and lady who are to partake of this grand fish which will delight our palates with tales of its life in the Pacific. Cheers."

We clink glasses, drink, and Massey says, "You some kind of poet?"

"No, that would be my friend, Gunnar Hoagart who humbly sits before you as Oregon's poet Laureate."

"No shit, you the Lariat?" Tillamook says.

"Yes."

"I like poetry some. You ever hear any of Robert Frost?"

"Oh, yes," Gunnar says, and then Tillamook recites "The Mending Wall" in a beautiful baritone.

"Wow, that was wonderful," Gunnar says.

"The old boy likes his poetry," Massey says. "Always has. Used to be that on lunch breaks, he'd set down on top of the hill, and pull some book of poetry from his lunch box."

"Yes I do." He finishes his glass of beer in one long swallow now as if the recitation has created an insatiable thirst in him. I fill everyone's glass.

"Now, who would like to try the first piece of steelhead late of the Wilson River?"

Massey and Tillamook look at each other, and then at the bartender whose name I learn, is Lil, and Massey reaches for a fork, stabs a piece of fish, and says, "I never eatin' no raw fish, but here goes." He dips it into the soy sauce, puts it in his mouth, and chews the tender meat. We all watch him in silence. He finishes chewing, swallows, furls his brow in some kind of culinary assessment, and then he stabs another piece of fish and repeats the process. When he reaches for a third, Tillamook says, "Now hold on there, boy, you got to save some for the rest of us," and he tries it and says, "Hey, that's not bad," to which Massey says, "I like it. I believe I like it." Lil, cuts a piece into tiny bits and gums it, and then Gunnar and I eat some until it's gone, and I have to go back out to the rig to cut another piece. We end up spending two hours and a quarter of a steelhead in this tavern on the Wilson River Highway, and it's three o'clock when we finally leave, Gunnar looking at his watch before saying, "I told you so. Didn't I? I told you we'd be late," and then we both laugh when Gunnar says, "Better late than never" because if we had never gone fishing on this glorious day, we would not have had the pleasure of dining with Massey, Tillamook and Lil.

When we cut off Highway 6 onto the road to Forest Grove, dusk is settling in for the evening, and I can both see and smell woodsmoke coming from the chimneys of the farm houses we pass. I turn up our drive, and I see two pairs of headlights just off the drive beneath the grove of filbert trees, and then I see the yellow crime tape, and then men standing in the dirt, flashlights moving, a woman writing something down. I hit the brakes, and skid to a stop, and I am out of the truck before Gunnar, and then I am there, standing above Bacchus who lies in a mess of blood, dead to this world, me watching myself react, falling to my knees, and I take her head into my lap, blooding myself, crying, heaving, Estuko there kneeling beside me, someone's hands on my shoulders, me holding Bacchus who has been shot to death on my property, my dog, my friend, my companion, Bacchus who was probably waiting at the end of the drive for me to come home so she could race me to the garage where we would sit together and share a couple of amber ales, Bacchus now dead, no longer a part of my world.

We're in the kitchen now. The police have promised to step up their investigation as they have warned us that this could become dangerous as the killer could be the same person/people as had put up the sign. It is more than possible, I feel.

Etsuko said she heard the shot and thought someone was out hunting as there are geese in the fields, but when she went out to call Bacchus in, she didn't come as she always did when one whistled her in in the evenings. She walked down the gravel drive, she said, and found Bacchus lying there barely alive.

She could see she wasn't going to make it. There was just too much blood, she said. She looked into her face with those pathetic brown eyes, and her chest heaved. She held her and told her *Good girl, good girl*, "...and she seemed to be comforted, Jake, she seemed at peace. I looked in her eyes and it was clear she knew she was going to die, and she looked at me as if she were saying goodbye. And you know what? She turned her head from side to side, and I know what it was she was doing. She was looking for you."

I'm across the kitchen table from her, and as I listen, warm tears slide down my cheeks. I am both full of remorse and full of anger and hate. If whoever did this were here now, I would kill him. That much I can say with surety. I would kill the son of a bitch.

We eat a somber dinner, and drink a little wine. Mother and Father are off to bed, and as I put my glass in the sink, Etsuko says, "Jake, let's go to bed."

"Yes. But I have to do one more thing."

"What's that?"

"I'm going to make sure no one is out there." I go to the closet by the back door, and I extract the Ithaca twelve gauge semi-automatic. Etsuko comes and wraps her arms around me.

"No, Jake. Stay here with me."

"I will. But first I am going to walk the grounds and make sure no one is out there."

"And if someone is?"

"I'll bring him in. Have him arrested for trespassing." I free myself of her arms.

"But if I have to, I'll shoot him."

"Jake, this isn't right."

"Well, it's the only thing I know to do. They killed Bacchus, Etsuko. Don't you understand? They are armed. They killed our dog. They could just as well kill us."

"Jake. Don't. Please. Don't go out there tonight."

I go to the door. I put on my down vest and a hat. I look at Estuko. "I love you. That's part of the reason I'm going out. And I love your parents. And I loved Bacchus. Probably no one is out there tonight. That doesn't matter. This is just something I've got to do." I open the door, cross the threshold, and close it tight behind me.

There is no moon tonight. The sky is clear, and it is cold, well below freezing. The stars are brilliant. I walk down the gravel drive and then I climb the hill where the grapes grow in long rows, themselves like spines. From the top of this hill, I can see a good mile of road, and there is no traffic. I stand here like a sentry, shifting my weight first from my left foot then to my right. The cold rises from the earth through the soles of my boots, up my calves and into my torso so that all of me is cold, cold and angry and sad. On any other night, Bacchus would be beside me, my companion, but now I am alone.

I see the headlights of a car approach. They move slowly, but when they reach the bottom of my drive, they continue without stopping, and I watch as the tail lights recede. In the next hour, only one more car approaches and ebbs, and I climb down the hill, and walk back up the drive to the house.

In the morning, Father helps me lift Bacchus into the pine box he and I have made, and we place the box into the back of the Jeep. Etsuko and Mother join us, and we drive down the path to the pond. It is raining hard and I have the wipers on as fast as they will go. I shift into four-wheel drive and we slide down the path toward the pond.

At the bottom of the hill, I park the Jeep and Father and I get out and remove the shovels. I show him where I want to dig on a small knoll on the other side of the pond. Bacchus liked to sun herself there whenever I was fishing for bass. We take the shovels in hand, and begin to dig the heavy clay soil. Though it is cold, and though the water has matted our hair and has run past our necks and down our backs, I can feel the perspiration break out on my forehead. When I stop digging, Father stops as well, and we stand with our hands atop our shovels, and we look down at the growing hole in the earth at our feet where we will place Bacchus for eternity.

It takes an hour to dig the hole, and then we place the coffin at the bottom and cover it with the dirt we have removed. When the hole is full and we have smoothed and tamped out the top, I go to the Jeep and get the piece of oak on which I have carved Bacchus' name and the following inscription: *She knew not how to hate.*

Mother and Etsuko join us at the side of the grave, and I say, "Bacchus, you will be greatly missed. You woke each morning with love and you carried it throughout the day until you went to sleep at night. We will miss all the days we had with you for each day you brought us joy. You personified what each of us should be. I will strive to be more like you and less like me, and if we all did so, well, the world would surely be a better place." And then I begin to cry so that Etusko puts her arms around me and leads me back to the Jeep, and she drives us back up the hill in the falling rain.

•

Finally, it is the morning of THE DINNER. Etsuko and Mother are in the kitchen, and the whole house has surrendered to the scents of their cooking. Father helps me set up the extra *kotatsu* in the tatami room, and then we work at setting places for eleven: Etsuko, Mother, Father, Elin (who arrived last night and who, upon learning of Bacchus' death, cried hard for an hour as first Etsuko and then I held her as she sobbed, for Bacchus was like a sister to her) and I, Karla and Gunnar, Milton the bailiff, and the three skinheads: Daniel Dunn, Keegan Porter and Leonard Harmon.

We have arranged the *kotatsu* as wings from the *hori-gotatsu,* and I tell Father that we will place both Leonard and Milton in the center as they are such large men and will need the extra space to stretch out their long legs. Last night, Elin made name tags to set in each person's place so that the seating arrangement appears as such: I am at the head and from my left are Gunnar, Karla, Leonard, Mother, and Keegan. From my right are Father, Elin, Milton, Daniel and Etsuko. It was Etsuko who made the seating arrangements and when I protested that I did not want Mother sitting next to a skinhead, she matter-of-factly said, "That is entirely the point of the dinner, Jake. We are to be in close proximity of these young men. Besides, if Leonard did anything to Mother, Karla would probably choke him to death." And though I laughed, I did not doubt the veracity of the statement.

It is snowing lightly and the garden is turning white. From the tatami room, I can see the waterfall. The pond has a thin sheen of ice over which the snow collects except where the waterfall meets the surface. It is a gray day with hints of blue, a day that pushes people inside. The flakes are small and they fall softly as the morning is still, not a hint of wind. I have made a fire in the living room, and if Bacchus were alive, she would be stretched out on the rug by the hearth lolling in the warmth. She would yawn and look up at me as I walk through the living room, but she would not get up unless I were to open the garage door off the kitchen. Then she would bound after me, thinking I was going for a walk. I used to throw snowballs for her to fetch, and if the snow were light, she would become confused when she bit into the ball and it fell apart so that there was nothing to retrieve. Then she would run around looking for a white ball in the white world, and she would become agitated so that I would call her back and make another phantom ball for her to fetch. Ah, I miss my Bacchus so very much. I do not understand the meanness of this world. Yet there are bumperstickers that profess the basest of beliefs, and the drivers are proud to be ignoble idiots. In response to the bumpersticker *Mean People Suck* I have seen *Nice People Suck*, and such a sensibility I do not understand. I continue to want to make the world nicer, more humane, and I fear such a desire may well be evidence of lunacy. Etsuko, too, suffers from this malady, and tonight her efforts may well render the two of us completely insane. I remember this from the Tao: *Give up Sainthood, renounce wisdom,/And it will be a hundred times better for everyone./Give up Kindness, renounce morality,/ And men will rediscover filial piety and love./Give up ingenuity, renounce profit,/And bandits and thieves will disappear./These three are outward forms alone; they are not sufficient in themselves./It is more important/To see the simplicity,/To realize one's true nature,/To cast off selfishness/And temper despair.*

But how to temper despair? How to run from the angst that is invisibly attached to the coccyx? It is as though when we were more feral animals without self-analysis there was no such thing as angst, but once our tail was evolutionarily severed from the coccyx, angst replaced it as an ironic joke suggesting that though we humans think we are superior because of our lack of tail, the angst that has replaced it will be a constant reminder that we are not.

Father and I are sitting at the kotatsu sipping green tea and eating mikan. We are content to be quiet and feel no need to talk as we watch the outside world being whitened by this morning snow shower. It is a beautiful sight. Soft and kind. I hear Etsuko call me from the kitchen, and I tell Father I will return in a minute. He merely nods his head and continues his gaze out the sliding glass doors. I wonder what he thinks today when we are having such guests for dinner. I know he is proud of his daughter and of his granddaughter, too, but he must also be worried as am I.

In the kitchen I find the two women hard at work. "Jake, will you run to the store for me. I thought I had another bottle of soy sauce, but I don't."

"Sure. Anything else I can get?"

Mother is rolling out dough for soba, buckwheat noodles that are a daily staple thought to be so medicinal that they are an integral dish on festive occasions such as New Year's Eve, the dolls' festival and memorial services. Mother is a strong woman, her arms rippled with muscles. She looks up at me and smiles, her gold tooth a sparkle of glee which reassures me.

Etsuko is stirring broth on the stove top. "No, nothing else."

I walk up to her and put my arms around her waist. I kiss her on the back of the neck, and I look at mother and see her blush. Etsuko says my name in a tone of warning, and I release her and go up and kiss Mother on the cheek and she puts up both doughy hands to ward me off, and she smiles, laughs and says my name as if it were a sigh. I walk to the door, take the keys from the hook, and as I open the door to the garage, I hear myself call for Bacchus. Both women look up at me and I stop still and shake my head. Then I am off, the door closed behind me, no dog in tow.

As I drive, the snow falls heavier as if it has decided that since it has started, this world might as well be completely whitened. I get on the freeway and drive slowly for this snow is wet as the temperature has yet to fall, and the roads are slippery. I take the exit, and pull off the highway and into the Safeway parking lot where there are few cars.

I go into the store and find the soy sauce, and then I see Dave behind the meat counter and I stop to say hello.

"Have you been back goose hunting?" He asks.

"No, but we went out duck hunting a week ago." I tell him about our trip to Sauvie Island, and when I tell him how Father painted his face with kanji, he laughs hard.

"That's a good one," he says. "He must be quite a character."

"Well, he really is. I never knew him well enough to know that, is all. But having him stay here this month has been wonderful. The more I get to know him, the more I like him. He cooked sukiyaki that night, and it was delicious."

"I bet it was. Did you see we have prime rib on sale?"

I laugh.

"What's so funny?"

I tell him how Etsuko told me she had told the aspiring poet and vegan at Portland State University the same thing, and how we had laughed, and now he laughs too. "Anyway, dinner's decided. Etsuko and her mother are making a traditional Japanese dinner. They're home now cooking up a storm."

"It looks to be a storm out there, from what I can see. What's the occasion tonight? Elin home?"

"She is. But it's not that." I tell him the story and how Etsuko wanted them sentenced to dinner, and he looks over the counter at me in a grave way. "What do you think?"

"I think you have a very smart wife. You are a lucky man."

"I am, Dave. I really am."

As I drive home, the snow is falling harder so that I have to turn my wipers on full speed, and I shift into four wheel drive. The temperature is dropping, and I am worried that the dinner will have to be canceled. I hope not, a sentiment I find funny because I never wanted the dinner in the first place, but so much effort has been made that I don't want to reschedule.

When I open the kitchen door, I again expect Bacchus to greet me. I find Etsuko and Mother rolling sushi at the counter and Father sitting at the table reading a book. "Where's Elin?" I ask.

"She's doing homework in her room," Etsuko says.

I come into the kitchen and set the soy sauce on the counter and ask if there is anything else I can do at the moment. Etsuko says I might put a log on the fire, and I say, "Sure. Then I think I'll ask Elin to go for a walk. It's been a long time since I've walked through the snow with my daughter."

I put two oak logs on the fire and close the screen. I look down at the rug I am standing on, the rug where Bacchus always lay, and I feel saddened, blue, and I wonder why blue is the color of dolor. Do we have a color for bliss? I wonder. Blue has always been my favorite color, and to an extent I have enjoyed the wallow through melancholy like James Joyce's Irish boy in love with Mangen's sister in "Araby," one of my favorite short stories. When you climb into melancholy and are thoroughly enveloped, you are safe from the abstract ether of angst.

I knock on Elin's door and hear her tell me to come in. "What are you studying?" I ask her.

She is sitting at her desk. She puts the book down. "I'm reading Kazuo Ishiguro's novel *The Unconsoled.*"

I sit on the bed. "What class?"

"Post-modern lit."

"You like the book?"

She purses her lips, then smiles. "Yes. It's absolutely frustrating, and I love it."

"He's a brilliant writer."

"He is, dad. It's funny what people think, though. I mean the other students. With a name like that, they think he's Japanese."

"I know."

"He's of Japanese descent, of course, was born there, but he grew up in England and he's a British writer. If we were reading a British writer named John Anderson, we wouldn't think he was Swedish."

"No."

"Anyway, I like him and I like this book."

"You want to take a break from studying? It's been a long time since I've had a walk in the snow. It's been a long time since I've had a walk with my daughter."

She stands, turns off the desk lamp. "Let's go."

Bundled up, we go out through the garage and I look at the leash that hangs from a hook, and then I look up and I see Elin looking at it, too. I reach out and touch it. When I turn, Elin comes into my arms and hugs me, and I feel the tears on my cheeks. We hug for a moment and then I kiss the top of her head, and then we go out into the falling snow hand in hand.

We take the path down to the pond. The snow is a couple of inches deep now, and we leave our footprints behind us waiting to be filled. "Bacchus loved to come down to the pond," I say.

"I know. I liked throwing sticks into the water and watching her leap and splash her way across."

"She loved fetching. And she was so social. Whenever we walked like this, she would run ahead but would always look back to make sure we were coming."

"Do you think they'll catch them?"

For a moment I am at loss and I say, "Who?" before I continue and say, "No, I don't think so."

I slip on the hill, but Elin holds my hand firmly, and I right myself. Our breath rides out on the words we speak before disappearing with their sound. "Do you think it was one of the boys who are coming tonight?"

"No. Just someone else who hates. Maybe one of their brethren. Too many people hate."

Elin stops and looks me full in the face. "Dad, I'm scared. Well, maybe not scared exactly, but nervous. About tonight."

I pull her into my arms and tell her she doesn't need to be afraid, that this is their sentencing, and, "Besides, Milton will be here. Nothing untoward is going to happen." I don't mention the shotguns.

She laughs and kisses me on the cheek. "*Untoward.* Oh, dad, sometimes you say the funniest things. As mom says, you are a funny man."

"Yes," I say. "But I don't feel so funny at the moment."

We arrive at the pond and circle it. There are three wood ducks swimming in the center where the water has yet to freeze. We break through the snow's crust onto the sedge that grows around the pond. We flush a hen pheasant and her roar of wings breaks through the silence of the falling snow. We both jump at the noise. My cheeks feel cold now, as does my nose. The walk is invigorating, as is the cold. I feel awake, mentally acute now, ready to tackle new tasks. I also feel rich and fulfilled as my daughter Elin is at my side, this wonderful girl a product of love with two different cultures in her wake. What occurs to me now is the poem "On Children" by Kahlil Gibran: *Your children are not your children./They are the sons and daughters of/Life's longing for itself./They come through you but not from you,/And though they are with you/yet they belong not to you./You may give them your love but not your thoughts,/For they have their own thoughts./You may house their bodies but not their souls,/For their souls dwell in the house of tomorrow,/which you cannot visit, not even/in your dreams./You may strive to be like them, but/seek not to make them like you./For life goes not backward nor tarries/ with yesterday.*

"Dad, what were you thinking? I lost you there for a moment."

We are walking back up the path. "Oh, I was thinking about the Gibran poem. "On Children.""

"The one on my wall."

"Yes, that one."

"Why?"

"I don't know. I guess because of you. I'm so happy you're here with me. You know something?"

"What?"

"I love you."

"I know that, silly. And do you know something else?"

"What?"

"I love you, too." She plants a quick kiss on my cheek and we walk home in a world growing white in the late afternoon falling of winter dusk, and I can only think of how lucky I am to have had my love for Etsuko manifested in Elin whom I love so much I could cry.

I am, indeed, a lucky man.

As I stand in the living room by the fire, I can see headlights coming up the drive through the falling snow, and as the car pulls into the drive, I recognize it to be Gunnar and Karla's. As I walk to the door to meet them, again I think of Bacchus for she would be at the door by now, barking and wagging her tail waiting to greet whomever was there. In fact, she would greet the son of a bitch who killed her with total equanimity. If she knew he was going to kill her, I am sure her reaction would be utter confusion, thinking *Now why would anyone want to kill me?* As I open the door, they both stamp their feet on the porch and come in and remove their shoes. "How are you holding up?" Karla asks me.

"Fine."

She hugs me, and then Gunnar does as well. "How about a Scotch to fortify ourselves before the onslaught?" I say as I lead them to the kitchen where there are more hugs. Karla even hugs Mother and Father, and they are both a bit stupefied by the embrace even though they've been hugged by both of these fine people for a couple of weeks now. Gunnar hugs them both as well, and I find myself thinking, what a fine greeting is a hug.

I mix drinks for everyone, and Karla joins in the culinary labor with Etsuko, Mother and Elin. With generous tumblers of Scotch, Gunnar, Father and I take refuge in the living room by the fire. The lights in the driveway are on, and from our seats we can look out and watch the snow swirl and fall, and we are engaged in a Japanese custom, *Yuki-misake*, literally drinking and watching the snow fall.

The three of us drink, look out the window, look at the fire, and are silent. What is there to say? It is as though we were awaiting some grave moment, a eulogy for a friend perhaps, and voicing our thoughts at this moment would be considered impious. But really, what is there to say? People are uncomfortable with silence, and I wonder why that is. What is so wrong with communal contemplation?

I hear the phone ring in the kitchen and all three of us turn in that direction. After a minute, Etsuko comes out to say that Milton has driven into a ditch about a mile away, and could we come to help pull them out? I get up and go to the phone and get the directions, and then all three of us men climb into my truck, and I shift into four wheel drive.

In the distance, Gunnar says he sees head lights, and then I see them, too, coming from a car askance in the ditch so that the lights shoot toward the sky, funneling snowflakes in their beams. As we approach, it is a strange sight: Three white skinheads behind the bumper pushing as a large black man sits behind the steering wheel gunning the throttle to no avail, yet shooting up snow spray from the rear wheels. I pull beside them and Gunnar rolls down the window. "You fellas need some help?" Gunnar asks.

The youngest boy, Keegan, replies, "Sure do."

I turn around and come up before the front bumper. Gunnar climbs out and attaches a tow cable from my tow knob and he hooks up Milton's car. I tell the boys to get out from behind the car, and after they do, I ease forward and pull Milton from the ditch. Once on the road, he gets out and inspects the side of the car where there is a small dent from the tree he came up against, but the damage is minor. Now we are all standing outside in the falling snow, and the three skinheads, who have been out the longest, are shifting their weight from one boot to another and clapping their hands in an effort to warm. "Let's get going and get inside where it's warm," I say, and we all load up and drive back to my house where four women, two Japanese, one Cherokee Indian and one part Japanese and part Caucasian await the arrival of the three of us in the truck and a large black man and three skinheads in the sedan. Sweet Jesus, I think, what a dinner party are we.

Except for Milton, Daniel, Leonard, Keegan and Mother, we are all seated in our assigned spots. Each of us is dressed in a kimono. Karla wears it well with her long black hair adrift on silk, but Gunnar looks stiff, awkward, iconoclastic. For some reason, I think of him holding his nose and saying, "*Cassoulet le bouchon.*" When he reaches for the tokuri of sake, his sleeves almost drag across the bowl of soy sauce. He is a poet clumsy with everything but words.

The lanterns in the garden are all turned on so that we can see the snow fall and rise from the ground in small drifts as the wind has picked up. We are warm in this *tatami* room sipping sake and waiting for the guests of honor. I find myself wishing that there are no guests, but I also find myself feeling proud of Etsuko for this grand if unusual attempt at amelioration.

Mother enters the room and looks beautiful in her gray kimono.

She smiles and flashes a twinkle of gold. She has her hair coiffed back with an alabaster barrette holding it in place. And then, through the door behind her, the kimono-clad men enter, first Milton who has to duck under the threshold, and then Daniel Dunn, the young man who seems most to despise us and even now he seems to sneer, then Leonard Harmon who sports an inscrutable smile as he enters, his cheeks puffed so that he looks like a squirrel storing his nuts, and then the red-headed and diminutive Keegan Porter who looks shy, bewildered even, as if he has been asleep only now to have awakened and upon finding himself in Japan, he wonders not only what to say, but also just how to say it.

Mother directs each boy to his seat, and they sit down. Strangely, I feel like this is the last supper and someone will be betrayed: Will it be Father, Elin, Milton, Daniel or Etsuko who flank my right in that order, or will it be Gunnar, Karla, Leonard, Mother or Keegan, who flank my left? And who will be the betrayer? I take a large sip of sake, and as I am about to speak, Etsuko stands. "Everyone, please stand now as I make the introductions." She then repeats this in Japanese, and now we are all standing up in our stocking feet, each of us wearing a kimono, the table laden with sundry dishes—*soba, udon, sunomono, otsumami, sukiyaki, tempura, tonkatsu,* various dried fish such as mackeral and squid, myriad sushi and sashimi, bowls of *sembei*, bowls of *edamame*, multifarious bottles of sake and beer and soda—so that the table is a virtual smorgasbord, and here we are, eleven people of four different racial backgrounds, of three different generations one of which survived World War II in its own front yard where the world's first atomic bombs were dropped, one Indian (she prefers this to Native American) who has seen her once fertile homeland flattened and paved, her people barely surviving an intended genocide, a renowned poet of Swedish extraction, a writer who hates three of his guests, three skinheads who hate everyone present save Gunnar and me, me who hates them the most, a large black man whose own racial history, his appropriation, his mere presence in a white world a seeming threat to so many whites, here we are to partake of a repast like no other, each of us dressed elegantly in a silk

148

kimono made by three of the women, all of us in a tatami room where we will sit on the floor and eat and drink as the falling snow outside the sliding glass doors reduces the outside world white, here we are now bowing to one another as Etsuko introduces Father to first Daniel, then Leonard and then Keegan, the three boys returning the bows on Milton's command, and in my own egocentric fashion the only thing I can think of is this: *There is no way in hell I could write this crazy scene. No fucking way.*

"Milton," she says, "I would like to introduce you to Karla Sweethorn. Karla, this is Milton Miles."

After the introductions have been made, we sit down, and I ask Etsuko to make a toast. She nods her head, and then she pours hot sake into Daniel and Keegan's cups while Mother does the same for Leonard and Milton, and I do the honors for Father, Karla, Gunnar and Elin. In Japan, one does not fill one's own cup, and Father fills one for me.

"Before we drink, I want to speak to why it is we are here." This she repeats in Japanese. She looks at Daniel, and then at Keegan and then Leonard before she looks at me and smiles, and I can feel her love from the other end of the table. Leonard and Keegan watch my wife with blank expressions, but Daniel, I see, still wears his superior sneer. I would like to choke him now, watch his eyes roll back into his head, and leave him dead on the tatami before continuing with our meal. Etusko seems to sense this in me, and she places her hand on Daniel's shoulder as if she were protecting him. He flinches, tries to take her hand off with his, but Milton places a firm hand at the back of his neck, and Daniel sits still and looks down at his steaming bowl of miso soup. So powerful is Milton, I can imagine him squeezing the punk's brain right out of his eye sockets. Or maybe that has already been done?

"We all know why we are here tonight." She repeats this in Japanese. "It is to help each one of us realize the humanity we all share together." She looks at Daniel, then Leonard, then at Keegan. Then she looks each one of us in the eyes, smiling the whole time. "There is a problem that exists still today, even though it has been some time since the incident in the Park Blocks when you three young men attacked me and my husband. You attacked us because you felt it wrong for him to be married to me, a Japanese woman, and I to him. But what you three do not understand is that I am no different than each of you except in appearance. I need what you need: I need love, and I need recognition and respect as a human. You must understand that I am no different than you. Nor is Milton, nor Karla, nor my mother or father, or my husband, or my daughter Elin."

"She's a half-breed," Daniel says, and I rise from my seat and try to go toward the kid, but Gunnar restrains me, and Milton has him by the back of the neck with his catcher's mitt of a right hand.

"Fuck you," Elin says to him. "Dad? I'm leaving," she says as she moves to stand.

Milton is squeezing Daniel by the nape of his neck and Leonard is watching with a huge grin. Daniel glares at him. Keegan looks at Elin with awe.

"Any more trouble from you, and you'll be back in jail," Milton tells him.

"Elin," Etsuko says. "I will not have that kind of language in this house. Now sit back down."

"But Mom," she starts to protest.

"Elin," Etsuko says with a stern countenance.

"Sorry," she says, and I smile for I am not in the least bit sorry. I remember when I was coaching Elin's basketball team, and we played against a team that played very dirty. When one of our girls was clotheslined by a player from the other team, Elin retaliated in kind, but she was careful enough to make sure the referee didn't see her. When she came back to the bench, I looked her hard in the eye and she shrugged and said, "Dirty laundry" which made me laugh at the time.

Etsuko resumes: "We seem to have a problem with communication. Daniel, you called my daughter a very insulting epithet, yet you do not even know her. But you hate her. Why?"

Daniel shrugs his shoulders, stares straight ahead.

"Because she is parts of different races?"

Daniel says nothing. Leonard sits across from him, nods and says, "Tell her, Daniel. Tell her why. She's part gook." Again he smiles vapidly. He is so obviously not the brains of their little operation.

Milton says, "Leonard, you say that word again, and you'll be locked outside like a dog. I'll chain you to a tree."

"What? Gook?"

Milton starts to rise and Leonard holds his hands out before him. "Sorry. I won't say it again."

Mother and Father look back and forth at the participants of what must seem an abstruse drama. Then they look at each other with eyebrows raised.

Etsuko continues: "Daniel, who taught you to hate? Please, I really want to know."

He turns to look at Etsuko and then at the rest of us. "Taught me? No one taught me." Then he smiles. "It just came naturally. Like bread and butter."

"Did your father hate? Is he the one?"

"No. Never knew him."

"Your mother then."

"She didn't have time to hate. She was drunk then and is drunk now. I told you, no one taught me."

"What about David Benchly, Daniel?" Leonard says eagerly. "He's taught us a lot." Leonard turns to Etsuko. "David Benchly taught us about the Third Reich and Hitler and Jews and stuff. He's a good teacher."

"Did he teach you to kill dogs?" I ask. I feel my body tense. I want to grab Daniel, choke him, my hands around his throat, squeezing, squeezing as hard as I can squeeze, watch his eyes go wide until his body falls limp from my hands.

I want to kill him.

"What dogs?" is all Daniel says.

Etsuko looks at me, but I say nothing. My heart is beating fast, each of my muscles taut. Etsuko waits for me. I drink my sake in one gulp. I nod at her. I let it go. Father refills my cup.

"Who is he?" Etsuko says.

"He's the head of our group, White Reign."

"Shut up, Leonard," Daniel says.

Meanwhile, Keegan looks on with little interest. I notice he does sneak looks at Elin from time to time, but I think the looks are not of hate born of white supremacy as much as they are the natural darting looks of a boy attracted to a pretty girl when the heart dictates action and the timid mind says wait.

"White Reign?" Etsuko says.

"Yep. That's us," Leonard continues unmindful of the threatening look he is receiving from Daniel.

"Leonard, did your parents teach you to hate?" Etsuko asks. We all defer to her as this is her show and it is opening night.

He picks up his glass of sake and takes a sip, looks at it and sets it back down. "Nah," he says. "I don't think so. Dad was always gone. He drives truck cross-country. Mom, she's a waitress at Jubitz. The truck stop. She always came home tired. Bad feet, she'd say. Nah, they never taught me to hate. But when I dropped out of high school, I hooked up with Daniel downtown and that's when we met David, and he taught us a whole bunch of stuff, didn't he, Daniel?"

Daniel glares at him even harder. "Well, damn, Daniel, what's got you tonight? You afraid to talk about David or something?"

"Mrs. Weedsong," Daniel says enunciating each syllable with precision. "Ignore Leonard. He is known to exaggerate. You ask where we learned to hate. I do not necessarily hate you. I only know that you are inferior to the white race, and that you should not be mixing with the white race as you will otherwise dilute our gene pool. It is better that you stay with your kind, and we stay with ours. You should go back to Japan."

"Etsuko, I've heard about all I care to from this little asshole," I say.

152

"From Daniel, Jake," Etsuko says. "*From Daniel.* And Leonard, you feel the same way?"

"Well, shoot, of course I do. That's what David says in a nut shell." Leonard smiles. He seems to be as malleable as clay.

Estuko turns to Keegan who has yet to speak. "And you, Keegan? What do you have to say?"

He looks at her and blushes, and then he looks across the table at Elin and goes redder yet. "I don't know, ma'am. I mean, what was the question?"

"Just where was it you learned to hate?"

"I don't hate anyone."

"But you're a white supremacist, right?"

He looks at Daniel and then at Leonard, and then back at Elin again who gives him a brief smile despite her present state. It is true, though: The boy is like a little puppy. "Yes, well, I don't know. I mean, well, I haven't been long with these fellas. I'm just kind of learning the ropes is all."

"And the ropes," I say, "had you attack us in the park? Kill our dog?"

He looks down at his lap, and then he looks back up at me. "I don't know anything about your dog, sir. But yes, it's true we attacked you, and for that I am sorry."

Daniel rolls his eyes. Leonard smiles. Etsuko reaches across the table and pats the boy's hands. "Let's begin eating," she says. "But first I would like Mother to give the boys a lesson eating with chopsticks."

"Chopsticks," Leonard says. "Wow. I've never tried. It must be hard."

"I'd prefer a fork," Daniel says. "It's a more modern invention."

"You'll use whatever the lady tells you to use," Milton tells him. "So pay attention."

In his effort to alleviate the tension, I think, Gunnar says to no one in particular, "Well, this should really be fun," and when I give him an incredulous look, he says, "Well, it will be, right?"

Mother stands and with two lacquered chopsticks, she demonstrates how to use them. Keegan pays close attention and follows each step with his own. Like everyone but the three young men, Milton knows how to use chopsticks and he helps instruct Daniel as does Etsuko. Karla works with Leonard, but it is slow going as his hands are big and soft like balls of dough, and he finds it difficult to manipulate the thin instruments that protrude from his hands like toothpicks from meatballs. I can see the fierce concentration in his furrowed brow. Sitting next to Keegan, Mother manipulates his fingers and in a few minutes he is picking the small pieces of tofu from his *misoshiru* with surprising dexterity so that mother smiles and pats him on the back like a young boy who's mastered a lesson.

I can see that Daniel takes pride in doing everything well, and though he is not as dexterous as Keegan, he lifts a piece of tofu from the soup but it slips and splashes back into the soup so that he goes back to retrieve it. If nothing else, he is tenacious in his ways, and that scares me: if he cannot be deprogrammed, he will continue on this frightful path of hate.

Leonard is now helping himself to thin slices of the duck sukiyaki that father has prepared, and he is holding his bowl of rice and shoveling in mouthfuls as Mother has shown him. Now everyone is busy eating and drinking, and it is as though the food is an elixir that has vanquished our memories of hate. The snow continues to fall softly outside and it is drifting higher so that there are several ribs of snow undulating into the darkness beyond the reach of the lantern light, waves of snow drifting out to sea. As I taste the sukiyaki, I smile at father and tell him it is delicious and I can see the pride in his eyes as he tells me that it is not bad, but that a better cook could have utilized such delicious duck in a far better manner.

"This food is incredible," Milton says as he helps himself to more of the shrimp tempura. "It reminds me of Yokosuka."

"You were in the navy?" I ask.

"Four years. Two of which I spent in Japan."

154

"Do you speak Japanese?" Etsuko asks.

"*Sakoshi-desu*," Milton replies. "Just a little. I'm not too good at languages, but I tell you what, I loved my time there."

"You were in the navy, huh?" Leonard says. "You like it?"

"I did. I saw a lot of the world and learned a lot and it paid for part of my education."

"Huh" is all Leonard says in reply, but I can see he is thinking something over. When he thinks, it is like he's driving a manual transmission with the gears far apart, stepping on the clutch and shifting from gear to gear, the synapses surprised at each shift.

Mother stands and walks over behind Elin and whispers something in her ear. Elin gets up and goes to sit in her place next to Keegan, and Mother sits down next to Father and pours him a glass of sake. In appearance, it seems she wanted to sit next to her husband and serve him, but I know she has something else in mind. I believe she sensed that Keegan would enjoy Elin's company, and I think Elin senses this as well, for now as she sits down she asks him how he enjoys the food, and he tells her it is delicious, and I watch her as she teaches him to say, "*Totemo oishii-desu*," which he then says to Etsuko who smiles and thanks him.

"Remember when you taught us how to say "*Cassoulet le bouchon*, Jake?" Karla holds her nose now and says it again. "Remember?"

"Of course."

She turns to Etsuko. "Etsuko, teach us all to say something like we did that night and we will go around the table and repeat it. Mother and Father can be the judges to see who has the best pronunciation."

Etsuko sets down her cup of hot sake and smiles. "Okay. What shall we say?"

"How about a haiku in Japanese?" Gunnar suggests.

"We could. Keegan? What would you like to say in Japanese?"

Keegan sets his chopsticks on the edge of his plate. He looks at Elin and blushes.

"I don't know," he says.

"How about "*Ohashi ga jyosu desu ne*," I say.

"What's that?" Gunnar asks.

"It means you use chopsticks well," Milton says. "It's a compliment."

"That's a good one," Leonard says through a mouthful of rice. He has mastered the technique of holding the rice bowl to his mouth and pushing the rice into his mouth with the coupled chopsticks.

Daniel says nothing. He seems hungry, though, but reluctant to show his hunger. He takes a piece of the duck to his mouth.

Etsuko says, "Jake is being a bit ironic, aren't you, Jake?"

Everyone looks at me. "I suppose a bit."

"Why?" Karla asks.

"It's because he heard that a few times in Japan. Once we were in Kyoto eating at a small out-of-the-way inn, and the cook came out of the kitchen to watch Jake eat. I don't think she had ever seen a *gaijin* before, let alone one who used chopsticks, and she said, "*Ohashi ga jyosu desu ne*. She was truly impressed a *gaijin* could use chopsticks so well."

"*Gaijin*?" Keegan asks.

"Foreigner," Milton says.

"Well?" Karla says. "Shall we? How does it go again?"

"*Ohashi ga jyosu desu ne*," Etsuko says. She goes on to tell both her mother and father that together they will be the judges of pronunciation.

Karla repeats it well: "*Ohashi ga jyosu desu ne*," she says.

"Well done, Karla," I say. "Now, let's go around the table and say it. Leonard?"

Leonard sets down his bowl of rice. He smiles. I swear to God, he smiles like this is the most fun he's had in ages, and I find myself thinking that if he had been raised in our household how very different he would now be. He looks at Etsuko. "Let me hear it one more time."

"*Ohashi ga jyosu desu ne*," Etsuko says.

"*Ohashi ga jesus des ne*," he says.

"Almost," I say.

"Good," Gunnar encourages.

"But leave out the Jesus," I continue.

"What?"

"It's *jyosu*, not jesus. With an O."

"Oh," Leonard says. "*Ohashi ga jyosu desu ne*," he says and smiles.

"Very well done," Etsuko says.

"*Sugoku ii hatsuon*," Mother compliments.

"What's that?" Leonard asks.

"She said you have good pronunciation," I say.

He beams.

"Now your turn," I say to Mother and she laughs, her mouth a gold twinkle, and she says the phrase, slowly articulating each syllable as if speaking to a child.

"No fair," Daniel says. "She should have to say it in English."

I look at Daniel in surprise. "True," I say. "It would seem she has home court advantage. Besides, she's one of the judges."

Etsuko smiles and tells her parents that they will have to say it in English. Mother covers her mouth with her hand in coy embarrassment, while Father agrees.

"Jake, would you teach them?" Etsuko asks.

I nod to Gunnar. "It seems I've been relieved of my teaching duties for some time. Gunnar? You're the man for this task."

"Okay," Gunnar says. "But I think Elin would be the better teacher."

"I'll do it," she says.

In Japanese, she says, "Grandfather, Grandmother, I am going to teach you how to say *ohashi ga jyosu desu ne* in English. Listen: You use choptsticks well. First you, Grandfather. You use chopsticks well."

He takes a sip of sake, sets his glass down. "You ooze chopstick well."

"Very good," Elin says.

"*Hatsuon ga jyosu desu ne*," Milton says and Father beams.

Elin turns to look at Mother. "Grandmother: You use chopsticks well."

She laughs and the gold sparkles in the candle light. Outside, it is snowing. "Okay," she says and blushes. "You use chawstick well."

Milton pats her on the back. Everyone save Daniel claps. Keegan looks at her and says, "*Ohashi ga jyosu desu ne*" to which she laughs and says "You use chawstick well."

Keegan repeats the phrase before Etsuko, sitting across the table from Keegan, tells him he has done it nicely. Then she, too, admires our ability to use chopsticks and now it is Daniel's turn. All eyes are on him.

He balks.

"Go ahead," Milton says. "Say it."

"No."

"Why not?" I ask.

"I don't want to."

"Well, if you are unable, then I'll say it," Milton says. "*Ohashi ga jyosu desu ne.*"

Then Elin, then me, then Gunnar.

"Now let's all say it together," Karla says. "On three. One, two, three."

"*Ohashi ga jyosu desu ne,*" we all, save Daniel, say. Everyone save Daniel laughs.

"That's good," Karla says. "Very good. Speaking another language is like traveling. Milton, where else did the Navy take you?"

"Australia, New Zealand, let's see, the Phillippines, Guam."

"Where was your favorite place?" Karla asks.

"Without a doubt, Japan." He smiles secretly and closes his eyes for a moment before opening them and saying, "Yep, Japan."

"What did you like so much about Japan?" Elin asks.

"Everything. The food. The people. The art. Everything." He helps himself to more sukiyaki, then eats a mouthful and follows it with a bite of rice. "Man, I love the food."

Mother, now sitting between Father and Milton, fills Milton's cup with sake, and he says, "*Domo arrigato gozaimasu*" before taking a drink. "Etsuko-san, thank you for having us over tonight. Everything is delicious."

"Yes," Gunnar says. "Everything is wonderful. As usual."

"Good, I'm glad. Keegan? Do you like the food?"

"Very much, thank you."

"And you, Leonard?"

Leonard is taking big bites of the pumpkin tempura. He wipes his mouth with the back of his hand. "Very good."

"Daniel? What about you?"

"It's okay. I like the shrimp some."

I would say that is true as he has eaten at least six of the big prawns. I pass him the plate of *ebi tempura* and he takes three more. "You do seem to have learned the art of using chopsticks rather quickly," I tell him and he shrugs his shoulders. "*Ohashi ga jyosu desu ne*," he says with excellent pronunciation.

Etsuko asks her parents who has the best pronunciation, and they confer in hushed whispers. They come to a verdict, and in Japanese, Father says, "It was very difficult. Each of you articulated the syllables with just timing, and correct stress. We have decided with great difficulty that the winner is Daniel-san."

Everyone claps. Daniel doesn't smile. With his chopsticks, he lifts a large deep fried prawn from his plate, and he eats.

I have never seen him smile. I doubt I ever will.

Leonard says, "Good job, Daniel. You win."

Daniel continues eating. I watch him and sigh. I look at Milton and for a moment our eyes tell each other what we both know: while maybe, just maybe, we have affected Keegan tonight, of Leonard we are less sure. He seems to go the way of the breeze. But, I think, each of us feels it is too late for Daniel. He has already set sail for distant and dangerous shores.

The competition over, we continue to eat. Dishes are passed, glasses filled, and Etsuko brings in hot green tea which, kneeling next to each guest, she pours into their cups. With the tea, we eat the bright orange mikan, their peels curled on our plates. It has stopped snowing, and the garden is quiet in the yellow lantern light. The waterfall pours gently into a small black hole through the snow-covered ice. Seeing the water fall into itself, it is as if we can hear its gentle nature.

The End

Timothy Schell is the winner of the Mammoth Book Award for Prose for his novel *The Drums of Africa* (2007) and is the co-author of *Mooring Against the Tide: Writing Fiction and Poetry* (Prentice Hall, 2007) and the co-editor of the anthology *A Writer's Country* (Prentice Hall, 2001). His fiction has been nominated for a Pushcart Award and he was the winner of the Martindale Award for Long Fiction. He teaches literature and writing at Columbia Gorge Community College in Hood River, Oregon. *The Memoir of Jake Weedsong* was the 2010 Finalist for the AWP Award for the Novel.

8750900R0

Made in the USA
Charleston, SC
11 July 2011